Also by Arnold B. Kanter
from Catbird Press

Advanced Law Firm Mismanagement
The Handbook of Law Firm Mismanagement

THE INS & OUTS

OF LAW FIRM

MISMANAGEMENT

A Behind-the-Scenes Look at Fairweather, Winters & Sommers

by

ARNOLD B. KANTER

Illustrated by Paul Hoffman

CATBIRD PRESS

CATBIRD PRESS, 16 Windsor Road, North Haven, CT 06473.
If you like this book and would like to see what else
we publish, please write us for our catalog.
A list of our humor books is at the back of this book.

Our books are distributed to the trade
by Independent Publishers Group.

Special thanks to the Sonnenschein people who helped with this book:
Barbara Handbury, Leon Henderson, Clinton Kinney,
Katy Kleinfeldt, Colleen McCarroll, Mary Raftelias,
Marv Schulgen, Errol Stone, and Karen Zydron.

Library of Congress Cataloging-in-Publication Data

Kanter, Arnold B., 1942-
The ins and outs of law firm mismanagement :
a behind-the-scenes look at Fairweather, Winters & Sommers
by Arnold B. Kanter ; illustrated by Paul Hoffman.
ISBN 0-945774-24-9 : $12.95
1. Law firms—Humor. 2. Lawyers—Humor. I. Title.
PS3561.A477I5   1994
813'.54—dc20   94-1381 CIP

For Clinton L. Kinney, former executive
director of administration at
Sonnenschein Nath & Rosenthal.
And for all the many people who toil behind
the scenes to make law firms the
great institutions that they are.

Contents

Introduction

ME AGAIN. Y'know, I never expected to get into the business of writing books about my law firm. Not that I'm not a gifted writer. In candor, I am. No Garcia Márquez, perhaps. But then *he* never had to survive the critiques of a pride of law school professors.

Not long ago, my publisher said to me, "Stanley (we're on a first-name basis, now), we've heard a lot about your firm's committees, but not much about the rest of the firm, how you get your work through the pipeline, out the door, through the fax machine, into commerce." Honesty compelled me to admit he had a point.

So we began knocking about ideas: he serving one up, me slicing it back. Me lobbing one over his head, he racing back to retrieve it. He dropping one short, me skidding to a stop as I reached it. Me going deep to the corner, he coming to the net. Pretty soon the possibility struck us that we might be playing tennis, not talking about a new book.

We sheathed our racquets and gave it another go. At first my publisher insisted on my writing the entire book. "Stanley," he pressed on me, "it's you who know most about the firm, how you get your work through the pipeline, out the door, through . . ."

"Yes," I admitted, "but others have important perspectives, as well. They've gained firsthand experience with both the nitty and the gritty of getting things through, out, into, over and between."

"I suppose you're right," he mused. "But experience is

an inefficient teacher. Maybe we can shortcut that process by asking some of your people to reveal the tricks of the trade as they've come to learn them."

"Hold it, let's not get carried away here. We don't want to promise readers something that useful. We haven't learned the tricks of the trade ourselves yet. But I'll bet people would love to hear the inside dope about lawyers from the folks who know them best. That much we could deliver."

"Capital idea, Old Sport," my publisher blurted, suddenly affecting a rather inexplicable British air. So, here we go.

Neither Rain Nor Sleet Nor Lawyers

By Harry Lopes

MAYBE I should introduce myself. I'm Harry Lopes, but everyone at the firm calls me "Hurry." That's because I'm always in one. A hurry that is. And I'm always pushing my corps to hurry, too. "Hurry along now," I'll tell them as I send them off on this or that mission.

We in the mailroom call each job we do a mission. That was my idea. Missions give people a sense of purpose. I think it all goes back to my days in Nam. When we went out into the field, we didn't go to do a job, we went out on a mission. Religious folks talk about that too, missions. Maybe it seems odd to you, people in our mailroom being out on missions. But everyone needs a sense of purpose in what they're doing, maybe especially people who aren't doing such high-falutin' stuff as our lawyers.

Anyway, I've been around our mailroom for a good long time now, so I've got plenty of good stories. Like the time some of our senior partners just about ransacked the mailroom. What happened was this.

Lots of clients write in to the firm every year to try to get their kids and relatives who are in law school hired by our firm. I guess each of 'em must think they're the only one with a kid in law school. Anyway, all of those letters were (at the time of this story I'm telling) sent to Otto Flack for him to answer, since he was the hiring partner. By the end of a hiring season, Mr. Flack got

pretty tired of answering those letters. One day Mr. Oscar
Winters got a copy of one of Otto's letters that read:

> February 24, 1978
> Ms. Shiela Kagan Grail
> 4200 N. Marine Drive
> Chicago, Illinois 60604

Dear Ms. Grail:

Thank you very much for your letter of February 22 to my
partner Oscar Winters.

As I understand Mr. Winters has already told you, we hire
very few first-year law students. This is especially true of
students from a lower rank law school such as yours. In candor,
I should tell you that we rarely consider hiring second- or third-
year students from your law school. In any case, we have
completed all of our first-year hiring for this year.

Since you are the daughter of the executive vice-president
of a pretty hefty client of ours, however, I'd be happy to spend
some time talking with you about next year. My candid advice to
you, however, is, if at all possible, try to transfer to Northwest-
ern or Chicago.

I note from your resume that you speak Spanish. Muy bien
(I speak a little myself). Frankly, however, that is of little use to
us since all of our clients speak English (most of them quite
fluently).

But, seriously now, I will look forward to hearing from you
and seeing you next year.

With kindest regards, I remain

> Yours sincerely,
>
> FAIRWEATHER, WINTERS
> & SOMMERS
> By: *Otto M. Flack*

cc: Mr. Oscar Winters

Now, Otto wasn't around the office when Mr. Winters got his copy of the letter, so Mr. Winters showed the letter to several of his partners. They all got pretty upset about the letter and came on down to the mailroom to try to find the original before it went out. Well, I'd never seen Mr. Winters or any of those other important partners down in the mailroom before, and especially not sorting through all of those envelopes in such a state of excitement. There was a fair amount of nasty language pronounced during all this, as I recall. One of the partners suggested that they'd better call Ms. Grail and make her an offer of employment right away.

After watching them for quite awhile, I asked them what they were looking for and Mr. Winters showed me the letter to Ms. Grail. I read it and laughed pretty hard. That got them awfully upset, and they asked what was so darn funny (as I recall, the word they used was not "darn"). I told them that I was sure the letter was a joke, that Mr. Flack hadn't sent the original. Well, it turned out I was right. And up until now I've honored Mr. Winters' request to never tell anybody about this, ever. In any event, Mr. Flack ceased being hiring partner quite suddenly, later that week.

But that's just one story about the things that go on in the mailroom. I could tell you many more, but I'd better get back to what we do, day to day—deal with the mail.

The mail isn't what it used to be. Do you remember the days when getting mail was a big deal, an event almost? Now what do we get in the mail? It ranges from unimportant to junk. Anything important seems to be faxed or sent by courier service, these days.

Of course that makes a difference for us in the mail-room. Nobody gets too excited anymore about whether the morning or afternoon mail is half an hour late. On the other hand, when something arrives by Fed Ex, I tell my messengers that they'd darn well better get out on a delivery mission pronto, or their rear ends may be astroturf.

We have our own parallels in the inner-office mail. In fact, recently we've made some changes in our internal mail delivery system. These changes are laid out in the memo you can read below, which I sent to all lawyers:

To: All Lawyers
From: Hurry Lopes
Re: New Mail Delivery Rules

Effective immediately, we are going to be switching to five classes of inner-office mail delivery:

- Book rate—in white envelopes. Delivery within two months, to the wrong office. No charge.
- Regular—in yellow envelopes. Delivery will be guaranteed by 5 P.M. on the second business day. No charge.
- Rush—in blue envelopes. Delivery within twenty-four hours if sent to somebody on the same floor as the sender, otherwise within thirty-six hours. No charge.
- Protect-your-ass memos—in brown envelopes. Delivery within one business day, return receipt requested. Fee of $5.
- Big rush—in green envelopes. Delivery within four hours. This will be handled by an outside courier service and the fee will vary from $10 on up, depending upon weight.
- Immediate delivery—in red envelopes. Delivery within fifteen minutes. If it's that darn important, drop it off yourself.

We believe that this new system will allow us in the mailroom to deliver the inner-office mail more efficiently. We will appreciate your cooperation.

Of course the Finance Committee was real pleased with our new policy. Less frequent delivery meant we could reduce the size of our messenger corps by one. Actually, we reduced it by two, because we let Old Sam go. We called Old Sam "Old Sam" because he was eighty-two years old.

The reason we were able to reduce the staff by two is that without Old Sam we didn't really need Young Sam. Young Sam's actual name was Jerry, but we called him Young Sam because his only job was to help Old Sam around. Old Sam was having a lot of trouble with his walking, and his eyesight was starting to go. Old Sam got a real nice retirement package from the firm. Yes, this firm may be getting hard-nosed financially, but one thing about it, it always takes care of its loyal Old Sams.

From time to time we've tried other ways to cut mail-room costs. A couple years ago, for instance, one of the partners got the notion that the firm was paying the postage on too many personal letters. At first the Executive Committee just circulated a memo reminding people that personal mail was not to be sent out at firm expense, but that didn't seem to have too much effect. So then they announced that all mail must be sent down to the mailroom unlicked. (Boy, that shows you how long I've been around this place—unlicked. Yessir, we used to actually lick envelopes closed, by tongue. Didn't care for hot, spicy foods much during that period. We had one fella who actually filed a workers' comp claim; said his tongue kept stickin' to the roof of his mouth. But there I go, off on another road altogether. Some folks say that's why I have to hurry like I do, 'cause I'm off on the wrong road so durn much.) But anyway, to handle that postage problem I was talkin' about, the firm hired two people to read all of the outgoing mail to determine whether it should be franked at firm expense or stamped "Return to Sender for Postage."

Naturally that created a few problems around this place. Several lawyers objected to what they claimed was an invasion of their privacy; some others said they were concerned about client confidentiality. Still others objected to the readers' suggested corrections of their writing style and spelling. And some others pointed out that the cost of the readers was eighteen times what the firm was saving on personal postage.

None of those objections would have made a difference, though, since it was no longer cost that mattered. Cutting out personal postage had become a great big moral issue for the Executive Committee.

What killed the mail reader experiment in the end was the trouble they had in defining what was a personal letter, which stumped even the Ad Hoc Committee on Personal Letters. That committee came up with the following definition:

> A personal letter shall mean any letter which: (a) contains more than 50% idle chit-chat, (b) begins with "My Dearest" or ends with "Yours 'Til Hell Freezes Over and All the Little Devils Go Ice Skating," (c) is addressed to Camp _____, (d) does not have a "cc" or "bcc" to anyone, or (e) does not begin with one of the following: "I have yours of the ____," "Enclosed herewith please find _____," "We represent XYZ Corporation," or "This letter will set forth our agreement with respect to . . ."

Though most folks at the firm agreed that the Ad Hoc Committee had made a commendable attempt, several lawyers pointed out how the definition they'd come up with both failed to include all personal mail (since some lawyers wrote personal letters that met all conditions in the definition) and was overly restrictive (since, for example, Rex Gladhand signed more than half of his letters to clients "Yours 'Til Hell Freezes Over and All the Little Devils Go Ice Skating.") So, eventually the effort to cut down on personal letters at firm expense through hiring readers was dropped, but the readers were kept on for two more years, until finally somebody noticed that their reading of all firm mail no longer served any purpose.

Those of us in the mailroom continue to be smack-dab in the middle of important firm issues. The hottest battle right now is over the question of whether all internal firm mail delivered by our messenger corps should require a stamp bearing the likeness of Stanley J. Fairweather. Personally, I think that's gonna happen. I told Stanley the other day that I thought he'd look real good on a stamp, and he said to me, "Y'know, Hurry, I believe you're right."

The Supply Side

IT'S NOT OFTEN that somebody from the Fairweather firm gets mentioned in the *Wall Street Journal*. And when that does happen, it's usually one of our lawyers, in connection with a case the firm is handling. Last year, however, the *Journal* profiled our director of supplies, Edward Johnston. We reprint that profile below.

Royalty in the Legal Supply World

Ed Johnston's Harvard Business School classmates don't chuckle anymore at the nickname they pinned on him at their fifth reunion—The Prince of Legal Pads. In fact, for his tenth HBS reunion this year, Johnston has announced that he's endowing a chair at his alma mater— to be known as the Ed Johnston Think-Small Chair of Entrepreneurship—at a cost to Johnston of $2 million.

Out of business school, Johnston had cast his lot with bulge-bracket investment bank Morgan Stanley. "Investment banking was what was hot, so I headed in that direction. In retrospect, I should have known better. Whenever too many Harvard Business School graduates are going into an industry, you can be sure that industry is headed down the tubes."

Johnston rode the bull market, and in three years he was making what he describes as "a fairly comfortable living in the low-to-mid six figures." When the market crashed in 1987, though, so did Johnston.

"I spent eight or nine months out of work," Johnston

recalls. "At first, I looked only at jobs in the salary range
and of the stature to which I had become accustomed.
After a while, though, I began to get more realistic."

Johnston says that he was talking to Ellen Jane
Ritton, an old college friend who had become a partner in
the prestigious law firm of Fairweather, Winters &
Sommers. Over drinks, Ellen Jane told Ed about the
problem her firm was having in hiring competent and
honest people to do some of the more routine jobs around
the firm. For example, she told Ed, the firm recently had
to fire its supply room head when it discovered that he
had been lifting supplies from the Fairweather inventory
and had opened up a small store in which he was selling
those supplies to the public. Ellen Jane admitted that the
firm probably would not have discovered the thefts had the
former supply room chief not chosen to name his business
The Fairweather Outlet Store.

As Ellen Jane laughed at the ridiculousness of her
firm's predicament, Ed told her that he wanted to apply
for the supply room job. Ed says that after Ellen Jane
realized he was not kidding, she looked at him as if he
were nuts. "I told Ellen Jane that I thought this was
preordained, I was just going from one Stanley to another,
from Morgan Stanley to Stanley Fairweather. The supply
room, as Ellen Jane described it to me, was in shambles.
This was a perfect turnaround situation, a classical case
study in the Harvard Business School mode. In short, the
perfect job for me."

Johnston says that his initial problem was dealing
with the Fairweather Supply Committee. "We spent most
of the first meeting I attended trying to decide whether to
get legal- or letter-sized legal pads. Some people liked the
fact that you could get more on a page of a legal-sized pad,
but others pointed out that the cost per line of a letter-
sized pad was actually less. Some thought that it was

important to continue with the legal-sized pads because 'otherwise, nobody would know you were a lawyer.' Still others preferred the letter-sized pad because it fits into more places more easily. We finally resolved to retain the legal-sized pads because the switch to letter-sized pads required a three-fifths vote, which the proponents of change on the Supply Committee couldn't muster. Thereafter, an effort to switch from yellow legal pads to white legal pads failed for the same reason." After sitting through that two-hour meeting, Johnston says he decided that thereafter he would make the decisions himself and seek ratification from the committee later.

Johnston says he discovered that the firm purchased most of its supplies by sending a messenger out to Ed and Moe's Top-Flight Office Supply Store, around the corner from the building. "When I saw Ed climb into his BMW one day, and Moe into his Mercedes 300SL, I figured that I had better start looking for special deals or sales to buy the firm's supplies," Johnston says. He also began saving money through buying supplies in bulk.

As part of the new purchasing regulations that Johnston established, the firm began to obtain at least three bids before ordering any supplies. To aid the firm in ordering the supplies, the corporate department drafted a simple form contract for use in all bids. A copy of that bid contract is set forth below:

Requisition Bid

The undersigned agrees to furnish to the Fairweather firm the number of items specified on Exhibit A hereto in the form attached as Exhibit B hereto (if the item is a desk or large machine, attach a photo rather than the item itself) by the date specified on Exhibit C hereto for the price specified on Exhibit D hereto if the Fairweather firm notifies the undersigned that this is the best deal they've gotten by the date specified on Exhibit E hereto. This bid is subject to all of the provisions of the Fairweather Standard Requisition Terms and Conditions, which are incorporated herein but which are too voluminous and onerous to attach hereto.

———————————

Signature of Bidder

Johnston says that once he got the purchasing under control, he turned to the use of supplies by lawyers. "I thought our lawyers were consuming much too much supplies, and that hunch was confirmed when I put our new requisition form [set forth below] into effect."

Fairweather Requisition Form

What do you want? _____

Do you really need it? _____

What do you need it for? _____

How many do you need? _____

Are you sure you need that many? _____

Why couldn't you get along on a couple less? _____

Check here to confirm that this is not for your kids' use in
   school. ___

   I hereby certify that, being fully aware of the firm's motto, "Waste not, want not," I still want the above supplies.

———————

Johnston reports that supply consumption was reduced by more than thirty-five percent after introduction of the new requisition form.

Johnston admits that his new purchasing procedures did not always work perfectly. "Sometimes we ordered too much, or ordered something that we found we really didn't need. When that happened, though, we just ran a sale to our lawyers and staff, and advertised it in the firm news-letter. We didn't make that much profit on those sales, but they were good for firm morale."

Not all of the firm's over-orders are handled so easily, however. Johnston recalls one situation in particular that caused a problem. "Our Space Committee had been considering a move to another office building for several years. They finally decided that we would move and were about to sign a lease, when I had to tell them that we had purchased so much stationery and business cards with our old address that the proposed move would be economically untenable."

Johnston says that by far his most successful decision was instituting a system by which the firm sells *all* supplies to its lawyers. "I figured we charge them for their soft drinks, why not for their legal pads?" says Johnston. To make the process easier, the firm issued Fairweather credit cards to all of its lawyers and promoted their use through advertisements in which Stanley Fairweather was pictured holding up the card, saying, "The Fairweather card, don't come to the firm without it."

Johnston's sales efforts at first met with opposition from firm lawyers, but have now become viewed as a perk. The firm will special order supplies for anyone, and delivers them either to the office or home (without charge, for orders of over $50).

Johnston says that the thing really took off when Fairweather clients got wind of his operation and began ordering supplies and wanting Fairweather cards. "We started making Fairweather credit cards available to clients, and pretty soon there was a demand to make the cards available to clients' friends. Eventually, we decided to just make the services available to the general public. We are now doing a thriving mail-order business," reports Johnston. "Cardholders who accumulate sufficient Fairweather frequent purchaser points may redeem them for free wills or house closings."

Recently, Ed Johnston went back to talk to his old friends at Morgan Stanley. But he's not looking to get his old job back. Gazing out over the city skyline from his new corner office at the Fairweather firm, Johnston told the *Journal* that the initial public offering of Fair-Mart common stock, which is being underwritten by Morgan Stanley, is due to become effective next week. At the estimated offering price, Johnston's holdings in Fair-Mart will be worth over $200 million. "I don't really mind being called The Prince of Legal Pads anymore," says Johnston.

Crime Does Not Pay

by Chief Brian Fitzpatrick

I'M A COP. Retired. But once a cop always a cop, I say. My beat—the Fairweather firm.

Now I don't wanna give you the idea that we got a lot of crime around dis place. But we got our share.

Lot of it is petty stuff. Usin' firm postage for poisonal letters, stealing from the supply room. But den a lot of da stuff that goes on around law firms is petty stuff, as most of youse lawyers knows.

Anyway, we figured we'd better nip this stuff in da bud, before it gets real ugly and outta hand. So dats why Mr. Stanley, he decide to hire me to fix things.

What's been goin' on around dis place lately is dis, and I wish you'd keep it under your hat, 'cause we don't want dis gettin' around, it might look bad, give the firm a bad name or sometin'.

This firm got a lot of departments, strong departments, tough departments. And dat's good. It helps da lawyers to have a sense of belongin' and it helps to organize da place, too.

But lately deez departments is gettin' outta hand.

We started pickin' dis up foist on da recruitment shift. One department's sayin' to a recruit, "You don't want to work for da tax department 'cause dey're a bunch of nurds." Dat may be true—in fact, in my poisonal opinion, it is—but we don't want dat spreadin' around, if you know what I mean. Ain't good for recruitin'.

Now, next thing ya know, da tax department gets

wind of dis and dey say to recruits, "You don't want to work for da litigation department 'cause all dey do is file papers and dey don't litigate anyway." Now, like I said before, this stuff may be true, too, and in my poisonal opinion it is. But you gotta keep a lid on dis stuff, for recruitin's sake.

Of course, pretty soon da litigation department, dey knockin' da corporate people to recruits, sayin', "Sure, you wanna spend your life doin' corporate minutes, you go right ahead and go to da corporate department. But utterwise, you come with us."

Now none of dis is doin' da firm no good at all, 'cause da recruits, dey not comin' to none of our departments. So at dis point, I fire off dis memo to Stanley:

To: Mr. Stanley
From: Chief Fitzpatrick

We gotta problem here, Mr. Stanley. Da boys in corporate and da boys in litigation is goin' at it again in recruitin'. I respectfully suggest dat we give 'em a jolt before dis gets too messy.

Stanley, he calls me in and tells me I better talk to alla' da department heads. So I go and say to dem, "Eh, what you guys doin'? You nuts or sometin'?" And I go on to explain da problem and to tell 'em dey better knock it off or we're gonna have ourselves a few little heads rollin' 'round. So, dey get da gist of what I mean, and we work ourselves out a little truce and dat pretty much puts an end to dat in recruitin'.

But just as I'm commencin' to think maybe I can relax a little, da next thing I hear is from da clients. Some of dem is complainin' about dere bills, and I'm hearin' dat da corporate department is telling dere clients dat da bills is too high because of dem litigation guys billing all dere travel time. Meanwhile I get wind dat some of da litigation guys is tellin' dere clients dat dere bills is too high 'cause da corporate guys is bringin' three guys to every meetin'. So I ask myself, "Eh, Brian, dis ain't good for business, is it?" And I answer, "No siree, you better go let Mr. Stanley in on what's goin' on." So I do, I send him dis memo:

To: Mr. Stanley
From: Chief Fitzpatrick

We gotta problem here, Mr. Stanley. Da boys in corporate and da boys in litigation is goin' at it again, and dis time it ain't recruitin', it's da clients. I respectfully suggest dat we give 'em a jolt before dis gets too messy.

So Mr. Stanley, he calls me into his office again and he says to me, "Hey Chief, you're right, you better take care of dis." So I try to take care of dis as delicately as possible, 'cause we don't want no blood spilled if we can help it, right? So I call dem in and I explain to dem about da facts of life and about how nice dere kneecaps look now, and pretty soon we got ourselves some peace again.

But it ain't over, dis bad blood between departments, 'cause you're not gonna believe what happens next. Some of da associates dey start to complain about how da firm's gettin' too big and dere not feeling like dey's a part of nuttin'.

To me, in my poisonal opinion, dis is a crock of you-know-what. I'd tell 'em to button up dere lips or go take a hike. But Mr. Stanley, he tells de department heads to work on dis problem and do sometin' about it.

And de department heads, dey do a good job. In fact, in my poisonal opinion, dey do too darn good a job. Dey make dere associates proud to be in dere departments all right. But dey make dem feel so proud dat dey commence to hasseling the associates in da utter departments.

Let me tell you what I mean. And here I gotta insist dat dis remain strictly confidential, 'cause it don't make us at da firm look none too good.

Nails Nuttree, da head of litigation, he gets his troops together. Dey start meeting in private. And dey give demselves a name, da LitiKings. Pretty soon dey start developin' secret words and secret handshakes. (I know dis, 'cause I'm listenin' in on my wire-tappin' device.) And dey develop a black LitiKings t-shirt with big gold letters on it.

Now maybe you're tinkin' this isn't soundin' so bad, but listen-up, here's what happens next. Da LitiKings announce dat dey don't want nobody from none of da utter departments comin' to dere floor unless dey got a pass signed by Nails Nuttree himself. Furthermore, da Liti-Kings start armin' demselves from da supply room with dem sharp staple removers and letter openers, and dey start flashing dose tings in a very threatinin' fashion in front of people in da utter departments. (I booked a couple of 'em on a 403(b), carrying a concealed staple remover, but dere out on bail, pendin' trial.) Not long after dat, LitiKings graffiti starts appearing all over da utter departments' floors, along with slogans like "Nails Lives" and "Depositions Forever."

Now, of course, you know da corporate guys ain't goin' to take dis lyin' down. So dey form dere own group, da CorpoMates, and next thing you know, at midnight one night, dey spring a surprise attack and take control of da duplicatin' department, and threaten not to let da utter departments use da darn Xerox machines.

Wait, I'm not through yet. Pretty soon da real estate department retaliates by announcin' in a six-page memo dat dey're not going to close no home deals for nobody in da utter departments.

In utter words, we got ourselves a full-blown gang warfare here at da Fairweather firm.

So I take da bull by da horns and I shoot off dis memo to Mr. Stanley:

To: Mr. Stanley
From: Chief Fitzpatrick

We gotta problem here, Mr. Stanley. You got gangs roamin' da halls of dis law firm. Dere ain't been no violence yet, but dat could change any minute. I respectfully suggest dat we give 'em a jolt before dis gets too messy.

So Mr. Stanley, he calls me in and he tells me to do sometin' about this gang problem.

I wish I could report to you dat we got dis ting completely in hand, but I can't. But we're makin' real progress. Here's what we're doin'.

First ting I do, I recruit me some law students to help out. I get dem hired by da Hiring Committee and infiltrate dem into alla da gang departments. From dem, I learn who da ring leaders of da LitiKings and CorpoMates are. I feed dat information into da Evaluation Committee and, before you know it, dees ringleaders start gettin' pretty bad reviews. At dis firm, though, we gotta read 'em dere rights about three different times before we can can 'em. If ya ask me, in my poisonal opinion, we got due process comin' out da wazoo.

But eventually deez warnins lead to several of dem gettin' fired. Unfortunately, however, at da Fairweather firm gettin' fired don't necessarily mean you leave da firm so quick. So most of dem are still around. Over time, though, I'm sure we're goin' to have dis problem solved.

Of course, dat don't mean dat other problems ain't gonna spring up. Probly dey will. But dat's what da Fairweather police force is for, fightin' crime wherever and however it appears. It's all in a day's work on the Fairweather beat.

Time Parts for No One

LIKE MOST FIRMS our size, we have not been spared the ravages wreaked by consultants. Excerpts from several of the reports written by our consulting firm, Tellem, Wathey, Noh, are scattered throughout this book. The one set forth below, written by name partner Dudley Tellem, relates to an evaluation of whether to permit attorneys to practice part-time at the firm.

Does the Firm Have a Part-time Policy?

This matter is not free from doubt, but the prevailing view seems to be "I think so." Opinions in the interviews I conducted ranged from "of course we do" to "no way, Jose."

There was a near-unanimous view that if the firm does have a part-time policy, it almost certainly is not in writing. Most lawyers I spoke to felt that the decision (if there was a decision) not to put the firm's part-time policy (if the firm has one) into writing was wise, since to do so might lock it in stone. None of those I spoke to favored locking the policy in stone, as this type of policy becomes exceedingly difficult to unlock.

Several felt that if locking in stone could be avoided, producing a written policy might be desirable, since then lawyers would know what the policy was. Others, however, thought that letting lawyers know what the policy was, if there was one, could lead to several problems. For one thing, if they knew that the firm had a part-time policy, lawyers might take advantage of that policy and this could make it difficult to get the firm's work done. Furthermore, if lawyers knew what the firm's part-time policy was, they might not (and, almost certainly, would not) like it and this could lead to unnecessary contentiousness.

What Is the Firm's Part-time Policy, If It Has One?

Most everyone thought that, if the firm had a part-time policy, it was a flexible one. Among other things, this meant that it was not locked in stone. As mentioned earlier in another context, this non-locking aspect of the flexible policy has widespread support among lawyers at the firm.

Some lawyers thought that the firm's policy was to handle part-time work requests on a case-by-case basis. Most thought that this was preferable to handling it on an every-other-case basis. While the case-by-case approach avoided stone-locking, it did raise problems of inconsistency and possible unfairness. Several pointed out, however, that consistency was not a feature of other firm policies either and that, therefore, the inconsistency itself represented a kind of consistency. Others opined that consistency was, in any event, the hobgoblin of small minds and that small minds was not what the firm wanted most to be known for.

As to possible unfairness, some thought that the same could be said of the firm's approach to associate evaluations, and to compensation and partnership decisions. Fairness, they pointed out, was in the eye of the beholder, much as beauty. Others noted that even life itself is unfair (citing many examples not here relevant).

Some lawyers thought that the firm's part-time policy was to allow each of the departments to make its own decisions as to whether to permit part-time work, depending on the needs of the department, the nature of the department's work, and the performance of the associate involved. Several thought, however, that the department's needs, the nature of the work, and the associate's performance were of considerably less importance in this decision than the whim of the department chair.

Many believed that part-time work would be permitted only in exceptional cases, the nature of which would be determined on a case-by-case basis. Others thought quite the opposite, that part-time work would be permitted unless prevented because of exceptional circumstances. Most thought that the decision in any particular case would be the same, regardless of which of the two standards were applied, since it depended upon the whim of the department chair.

What Factors Should Govern the Firm's Part-time Policy If the Firm Should Have One?

Here there seemed to be a clear difference of opinion. Partners felt that the firm's part-time policy should be governed by what was best for the firm. Associates thought that the firm's part-time policy should be governed by what's best for the individual, unless that would create a serious problem for the firm. Several partners pointed out that what was best for the firm was also in the long run best for the individuals. Several associates pointed out that this was preposterous.

What Are the Advantages/Disadvantages of a Part-time Policy?

Many thought that having a liberal part-time policy would provide an advantage to the firm in recruiting top law students. Others thought that this would be true only among students who themselves wanted to be part-time lawyers, and queried whether those law students were the type the firm ought to be seeking anyway, alluding to the outrageous salaries paid to law students these days, and all.

Proponents of a part-time policy argued that it would help the firm retain people who, because of temporary obligations, needed to work part-time. Opponents pointed out that those people could always leave the firm and apply to be reinstated at such time as they were prepared to work full-time. Proponents pointed out that there would then be no guarantee to those people that they would be rehired. Opponents said that's right. Proponents argued that those people might then leave and go to another firm. Opponents said that the market being what it was, those people would have difficulty finding work elsewhere and, if they could, God bless them. Proponents protested that that view was extremely short-sighted, and also assumed the existence of God. Opponents insisted that short-sightedness was a basic tenet of all firm decisions, and that they were pretty sure that God existed, though he/she might take different forms to different people.

Some argued that part-time lawyers would provide an economic benefit to the firm, since their salaries would be lower proportionally than those who were at the firm full-time. They also pointed out that most of the firm's many type-A lawyers would be unable to work less than full-time, even if they were paid only part-time.

Opponents asserted that it would be difficult, if not impossible, to manage part-time work. Clients were demanding and would not stand for lawyers not being available when they needed them. Proponents argued that this was only a matter of managing better. After all, lawyers went on vacation and somehow clients managed to get along without them. Opponents said that they had not been on vacation in five years. Proponents said that they had no one to blame for that but themselves. Opponents suggested that maybe if the Proponents worked a little harder it would be easier for them (the Opponents) to take vacations. The consultant cut off this line of debate, as it was getting ugly.

Opponents said that working part-time showed a lack of commitment to the practice that was inconsistent with being a big-firm lawyer. They cited as examples the fact that all of them had always worked full-time. Besides, if the firm adopted a liberal part-time policy, everyone would want to take advantage of it and "you can't practice law that way." Proponents argued that a system could be devised to allocate part-time work requests. Opponents asserted that such a system would be too complicated for people to understand. Proponents pointed out that, if this were true, there could be no question raised as to the system's fairness. Opponents begged to differ, arguing that firm lawyers were perfectly capable of challenging the fairness of policies they did not understand, and had done so many times in the past.

Recommendations

This is a complicated issue on which opinion within the firm is sharply divided. Both sides seem to have their strong and weak points, which I have tried to present impartially above. In situations such as this, it is best not to act precipitously. Certainly it would be very risky for me as a consultant to mix in. I therefore recommend that the firm give this matter a lot of further study. In particular, you may want to send a written survey to your lawyers so as to give them all an opportunity to be heard. For a hefty fee, I would be happy to conduct this survey and report on the results. For an additional fee, you may also want to have me conduct a study of what other firms have done in comparable positions so as to avoid the possibility, however remote, that you would be breaking new ground with your decision.

If you would like to discuss, at greater length, anything contained in this report, you must be out of your
minds.

An Organizational Overview

By Lt. Colonel Clinton L. Hargraves, CPA, CFO

FIRST let me say that I consider it an honor to be asked to write an overview for this particular book, *The Ins & Outs of Law Firm Mismanagement.* As a former accountant and military man, I have a certain natural literary bent. And since assuming the post of administrator of the firm, later promoted (on the basis of merit) to the title of director of administration, then to executive director, and finally to chief financial officer, the post to which I have now ascended, I have attempted to spit-polish my linguistical aptitude even brighter by circulating frequent memoranda on topics of interest to non-lawyers and lawyers alike at the firm with clocklike regularity. This increases the comfort level I feel in assuming this present literary endeavor.

Though I'm an army man, I prefer to liken the organization of a law firm to a large ship, or boat. At the helm, you've got the captain; in the case of our fine firm, Stanley J. Fairweather. The captain has the primary responsibility for setting the ship's course, providing a steady hand on the wheel (or however you steer one of those big boats; I told you I'm not a navy man) and keeping 'er "steady as she goes," unless you don't want 'er to go steady, in which case you've got to tilt 'er to the port or starboard, as the case may be.

And there are plenty of other nautical-like characteristics of law firm organization, too. There are the

partners, who would be your officer corps—admirals,
second mates and the like—and associates, who might be
thought of as your deckhands. And don't forget the folks in
the galley, our fine food service department here at the
firm, or those manning the lifeboats, our employee benefits
department. Down in the boiler room we've got our photocopy department, and up in the lookout, there's . . . well,
let's say business development.

Actually, it turns out that a law firm is not that much
like a ship after all. Maybe it's more like a shopping mall.

But in any case, organization is key to a law firm.
Without organization, you've got duplication of functionali-
ties, multiplication of expenditures, and non-optimization
of resources. In short, what you've got is disorganization.
And it doesn't take any chief financial officer worth his
salt very long to recognize that those eventualities are not
contributory to the overall health of the firm's body.

Come to think of it, the firm may be a lot more like
a human body than a shopping mall. Stanley Fairweather
would be its brains. No, perhaps its heart. Or its guts.
Maybe lifeblood. Never mind.

Of course, there are many different ways to organize
a firm. Some of those methodologies will be preferential to
one firm and others to another firm. So the exact method
of organization—or organizational method—that you
choose is not important. Well, it *is* important, but you may
choose from a large number of alternatives, some of which
may be better than others and others may not. The
important thing, I would say, is to pick an organizational
structure and stick with it as long as it is working for you,
and when it stops, change it, if you still can. Also make
darn sure you have one or more organizational charts.

At the Fairweather firm, we are organized from the
top on down, in sort of a pyramid. At the same time, we
have a strong centralized system which somewhat resem-

bles our own fine solar system. The diagram below is depictatory of those organizational models.

As you can see, in either case, the locus of control is fairly well identified.

As a lieutenant colonel (retired), I can attest to the importance of clear lines of authority. As a CPA, I can attest to the importance of attention to detail, counting every last bean. I have attempted to incorporate these important values into the organizational structure of our fine firm.

Let me give you some for-instances. For instance, we have both solid-line and dotted-line reporting responsibilities in our firm. It's very important to have both of these and to distinguish clearly between them, though no consultant I've consulted knows exactly why.

Another for-instance is this. As to bean counting, we try to watch every dollar that we spend, on the theory that the less of it that goes out, the more of it we've got left in here for ourselves. To help us watch, we try to set up a lot of controls, and checks and balances.

On the control side, any expenditure of $2.83 or more requires approval of a committee, incorporation into a budget line item, a signed receipt, and the completion of a detailed form that must be witnessed by three people and notarized. We feel that the small administrative burden this imposes is more than offset by the discouragement this procedure provides from spending anything, ever.

On the checks and balances side, we try to look over one another's shoulders in a friendly way, to make sure that nothing accidentally gets stolen. An unexpected side benefit of this is that the videos produced by the hidden cameras in our accounting department have provided hours of viewing entertainment for those of us on the Financial Oversight Committee.

I can speak most authoritatively regarding the organization of the support staff, all of whom report to me, either on a dotted- or a non-dotted-line basis, and some of them on both. As a lieutenant colonel (retired), I can attest to the importance of loyalty. When you're at war, you want to know that the fellow (or gal) behind you is going to cover your fire. And remember, in a large law firm, you are always at war.

One way I have attempted to increase the loyalty component of my troops is by hiring from within. Whenever a position becomes available, I make that job availability known to everyone through use of the Official Job Availability Notification Form.

Morale has increased markedly in the last year, since over seventy percent of the jobs available were filled by hiring from within. The morale improvement quotient was impaired somewhat, however, by the fact that most of the jobs filled from within were created by firing from within. But then you can't have everything, can you?

I believe strongly that if you want your departments to be operating at full throttle, you must give each manager of a department credit for the performance of their department, especially for their failures. I encourage my managers to build the same esprit de corps among their department members as I do among my management team. Very few fail to achieve or exceed that goal.

If your law firm is to function like a well-oiled machine, you will need regular interaction among departments and also between lawyers and the various departments. To achieve what I like to call OIP, optimum interaction potentiality, our firm has taken two steps. First, we have established the following designated interaction opportunity areas:
1. the halls
2. the building lobby
3. the elevators
4. the fire escape
5. the washrooms

6. the line waiting for your photocopy job to finally be
   completed

Second, we have appointed liaisons between lawyers
and each of the firm departments. A recent study of our
interaction accomplishments conducted for us by our
consultants, Tellem, Wathey, Noh, came to the conclusion
that "this necessary interaction won't happen, so you
might as well forget about it." Reluctantly, we have.

While I could easily go on at great length with this
overview, I have been allocated only limited space and
cautioned to be concise. Hence, let me conclude by saying
that as both a lieutenant colonel (retired) and a CPA, I can
attest that unless you focus carefully on organization, it's
darn easy to lapse into disorganization.

Nintendo for Lawyers

COMPUTER SERVICES at Fairweather, Winters & Sommers has grown from a tiny one-station operation to a vast network. The system is operated under the constant, watchful stare of Computer Czar Stevie Zwinga. This far-ranging interview with Stevie was conducted by ace Fairweather reporter and real-estate paralegal Loretta Stikes and originally appeared in the November 1993 issue of the Fairweather, Winters & Sommers newsletter, the *Fairweather Free-for-All Press*. It is reprinted here with permission.

Loretta: Stevie, thank you for taking time out of your busy schedule to talk with the *Free-for-All Press*.

Stevie: Hey, man, what's happenin'?

Loretta: If you don't mind, Stevie, I'd like to start with a little personal background.

Stevie: No, man, go right ahead. Tell me about yourself.

Loretta: No, I meant about you, Stevie. I think our readers would be interested in knowing something about you.

Stevie: Sure, man, happy to. What'd they like to know?

Loretta: How about starting with your childhood?

Stevie: Zingo, far out.

Loretta: What do you mean, "zingo, far out"?

Stevie: Technically "zingo" means either "great idea" or "exactly," and the "far out" is generally just added for emphasis.

Loretta: Well, could you tell us something about your childhood?

Stevie: No. — Only kidding, sure I could. Would you like me to start in the fifth grade?

Loretta: That would be fine.

Stevie: Actually I can't. I skipped fifth grade.

Loretta: Well, then how about fourth or sixth?

Stevie: Don't remember much about those. It was quite a while ago, you know.

Loretta: Maybe we can approach this differently . . .

Stevie: Yes, let's.

Loretta: How did you get interested in computers?

Stevie: Games.

Loretta: So you got interested in computers through computer games?

Stevie: Zingo. Nintendo, zapped them buggers, beep beep beep, ping; beep beep beep, ping.

Loretta: But how did you get interested in the operation of computers?

Stevie: Taking 'em apart.

Loretta: So you just took them apart and put them back together again? Amazing. Did you have any help?

Stevie: Well, my father . . .

Loretta: Your father helped you put them together? Was he in the computer business?

Stevie: Not exactly. He was a professional wrestler, and he told me that if I didn't put the damn computer back together again, he'd split my ignorant head open. I believe that's how Dad put it.

Loretta: Oh, I see. Stevie, a lot of us are pretty unsophisticated as to how computers work. Could you give us a simple explanation?

Stevie: Sure, you got your MS-DOS, your application and system software; you stick 'em into your hardware with RAM and about a thousand zigabytes of memory, stick in your floppy disk, hook up the modem, turn on the electricity, boot 'er up, and let those electrons loose, on-line.

Loretta: Thanks a lot, Stevie. Can you explain to us why the computers are kept in a glass-enclosed sealed room? Is this because they are highly sensitive to changes in temperature and to dust particles?

Stevie: No, man, that's just a myth that's been laid out there by computer experts around the world. Those computers are metal, man. You can smash those babies with sledge hammers and dump sand all over them, won't hurt nothin'. No, the real reason for these rooms is so that computer systems engineers can get a little peace and quiet, and not be bothered by stupid questions from computer illiterate people around the firm, like yourself.

Loretta: I appreciate your honesty, Stevie.

Stevie: Hey, don't mention it, man.

Loretta: Can you give us an overview of the computer operations that you supervise at the firm?

Stevie: Hey, why not, man. First of all, we've got word processing, which we now have networked and accessible at all secretarial stations and from lawyers' computers in their offices.

Loretta: So that everybody can have access to any document that's on the system?

Stevie: Theoretically no, but practically yes.

Loretta: What do you mean by that?

Stevie: Well, theoretically you need the password or code number of any attorney to get into his or her document base.

Loretta: Well, why is that only theoretical?

Stevie: Because every attorney uses his or her birthdate or their dog's name, so if you know those, their document list is an open book.

Loretta: Really?

Stevie: Yeah, really. You want to read some of Percifal Snikkety's erotic poetry? Let's punch in his name, his birthdate—January 23, 1938—and wammo, what have we here?

Loretta: Oh my God, I had no idea!

Stevie: Yes, I think this one on love in chains is particularly sensitively done, don't you?

Loretta: I don't think we should be doing this, should we?

Stevie: Of course not, but hey, you've gotta have a little fun somehow, don't you? All work and no play makes Stevie a dull boy, you know.

Loretta: Well, shouldn't we warn our attorneys about this?

Stevie: Not really. All they'd do is put in their spouse's or kids' birthdays—some of the more creative ones have done that already—and with the firm facebook, that wouldn't be any more difficult to access. Besides, only me, you, and a few others know about this, so it's no big deal. It'll be our little secret.

Loretta: But this gives you enormous power over all the attorneys, doesn't it?

Stevie: Zingo. For example, Lionel Hartz is on the Personnel Compensation Committee, and I've been quite satisfied with my salary increases and bonuses recently.

Loretta: Well, what about the other aspects of your work, besides word processing?

Stevie: Well, our computer system also controls all of the time records, billings, accounts receivable and payable—essentially all of the financial information about the firm.

Loretta: So that means you know as much about the firm's finances as the partners?

Stevie: No.

Loretta: But I thought you have access to all of the financial information of the firm.

Stevie: I do. But none of the partners except Stanley has access to that information. He thinks it would be much too dangerous for them to have it. Besides, most of them wouldn't understand it, anyway.

Loretta: But you generate all of those reports for the Finance Committee and the partnership, don't you?

Stevie: Zingo, that was Stanley's idea. Flood them with so much useless information that they can't possibly absorb it all. It's the same technique that Nails Nuttree uses in producing rooms full of documents to the opposing side in litigation.

Loretta: But I thought all of those financial reports were highly confidential.

Stevie: Of course they are, man. When did you ever see anything circulate around the firm that wasn't marked "Confidential"? If you really want to keep something a secret around here, you just circulate it without an envelope and with no indication of confidentiality. Then nobody will think it's important enough to read.

Loretta: Well, I know our computer operation has grown tremendously under you, Stevie. What do you see as the future for computer services at the firm?

Stevie: I see us getting a lot more into espionage, man.

Loretta: Espionage? You mean like in those spy novels?

Stevie: Zingo. Law is getting to be a tough business, man. Firms have got to invent new ways to compete.

Loretta: How would espionage help the firm to compete?

Stevie: You've got to be kidding, man. Can you imagine tapping into other firms' form files and billing information, stealing drafts of memoranda that they prepare before going into negotiations or court, gumming up their computer operations?

Loretta: What do you mean gumming up?

Stevie: I mean wiping out documents, decreasing their bill-

ing amounts by one zero, inserting strategic "nots" in
their documents. In short, creating a dread Fairweather virus.

Loretta: Mr. Fairweather would never go for that type of
behavior. And even if he did, how would you know
how to do all that?

Stevie: Oh, I've had a little experience with that, man.

Loretta: Experience? You mean you were a . . . hacker?

Stevie: Zingo. That's how the firm found me.

Loretta: How?

Stevie: Sheldon Horvitz represented me, pro bono. He did
a pretty good job. Kept me out of the can, and I'm
just finishing up my second and last year of proba-
tion.

Loretta: Well, I'm sure we won't get into espionage. But is
there anything else you see for us in the future?

Stevie: Sure, man, I see us getting more into computer
games.

Loretta: Computer games?

Stevie: Sure, man, most of our lawyers play them on their
computers now, anyway. Why shouldn't we create our
own instructional video games?

Loretta: Such as?

Stevie: Well, I'd call one of them "Widow." You'd see this
old biddy come wobblin' onto the screen, plop herself
down in a fancy law office, and ask to change her
will. If the lawyer playing the game makes a bad
suggestion, the old lady jumps out of her seat and
starts cursing at him. Hell, I'll bet we could even
work out some CLE credit for the games. And we
could market them to other firms, make a little dough
on them.

Loretta: That would certainly make the Finance Committee happy. And I guess that if we got into lawyer
computer games, you'd have come full circle back to

what got you interested in computers in the first place, Stevie.

Stevie: Zingo.

Uh-huh, I See

LAW HAS BECOME an increasingly stressful profession. In recognition of that fact, Fairweather, Winters & Sommers—being the progressive law firm it is—has hired a firm psychiatrist, Dr. Helpem Fielgud of Dusseldorf, Germany.

Dr. Fielgud first came to the Fairweather firm some four years ago, as a result of a wave of events in which several Fairweather lawyers exhibited some rather aberrational behavior. The first incident involved Hector A. Morgan and Rebecca Avridge showing up for a Court of Appeals argument dressed, respectively, as Daisy and Daffy Duck. The judge had to adjourn the hearing because he couldn't make out their oral argument, which he said "sounded like a whole lot of quacking." The second incident, which occurred only two weeks later, found Helen Laser leading three associates in a rendition of "When the Red Red Robin Comes Bob Bob Bobbin' Along" at the closing of a $35 million loan agreement, and then insisting that worms be served at the closing lunch.

Several Executive Committee members thought it premature to take any action based on only a couple episodes that were not much worse than many that occurred on a daily basis at the firm. The majority of the committee disagreed, however, pointing to the cross-dressing of Hector and Rebecca as being particularly distressing. And so the Executive Committee decided to authorize an extensive international search for a firm shrink to help Fairweather lawyers deal with the stress they were encountering. This led ultimately to the hiring of Dr. Fielgud.

Dr. Fielgud is a highly trained professional, having studied under the late Dr. Freud in Vienna. (In fact, Dr. Fielgud's mentor, Marvin Freud, is still practicing in Vienna. Marv is known as "the late Dr. Freud" because of his habitual tardiness.)

As part of its arrangement with Dr. Fielgud, the firm foots the bill for all of his sessions with Fairweather lawyers and provides Dr. Fielgud with a suite of offices, rent free. While Dr. Fielgud's sessions, of course, are strictly confidential, they are all taped and transcribed. This procedure is followed because Dr. Fielgud is unable to take notes. As he puts it, "I could get ink or lead on my hands und I vould die." The following is a transcript of one of Dr. Fielgud's recent sessions with a Fairweather, Winters & Sommers partner.

"Good afternoon, Dr. Fielgud."

"Yes, go on."

"Well, Dr. Fielgud, since the last time I saw you, things have not gone so well. I'm starting to have feelings of inadequacy. My biggest client, Accidental Insurance, is threatening to go to another law firm. They seem to be unhappy about the $2.3 billion judgment that was entered against them in a case we handled. I tried to explain that that type of thing can happen to anybody, but they pointed out that perhaps it was not very good advice we gave them in recommending that they reject a $20,000 settlement offer on the eve of trial. I'm not sure what I'll do if they leave."

"Uh-huh."

"And my new business development efforts have been a flop. My speech to the bar association committee on 'The Rule Against Perpetuities: Does It Still Speak to Us with Passion Today?' is unlikely to generate much business, since it was attended by only six people, including my wife and three children. None of my old college classmates, who I contacted to try to generate business, admit to remembering me in college. And I am the only person ever defeated for my town's zoning board of appeals, running unopposed."

"I see."

"Not only that, but my own partners don't seem to value me very highly, either. Our new proposed compensation figures have me taking a thirty percent cut in my piece of the pie, which is to be distributed equally to three younger partners in my department. I found out about the new compensation proposal from my secretary, who heard it from somebody in the duplicating department. I've tried to get in to see Stanley Fairweather about the compensation issue, but his secretary, Bertha, tells me that he is too busy this week and then will be on vacation for a month, by which time the compensation decisions will be final."

"Yes, and . . ."

"The two associates I work most closely with have each come in to let me know that they are planning to leave the firm. One of them, Brian Fitzmorris, is leaving to become general counsel for a client for whom our firm has been doing a lot of work. Brian tells me that he'd love to see me and my wife Alma socially, but he expects that he will be doing most of the client's work, in house. The other associate, Katie Wranch, told me that she wants to get closer to the action in real estate, so she is leaving the firm to buy a farm and grow alfalfa in Kansas."

"Uh-huh."

"My older son, Johnny, has decided that he needs to earn some money. In a way, I guess that's good. It's nice to see a fifteen-year-old who doesn't want to just take dough from his old man. Unfortunately, the reason he needs to raise the money is because he has a little bit of a drug problem. And I wish Johnny would consider another method of raising the money, instead of the weekly floating crap game he has established in our garage, basement, and attic. But basically I think he's a good kid and I don't think Johnny is serious in his threat to turn Alma and me into the IRS for failure to pay social security on our housekeeper's salary if we interfere with his crap game."

"I see."

"And speaking of Alma, well she is sort of talking about leaving me. It's not that we had that great a marriage anyway, since she's always told me that I bored her to tears, but it is a bit embarrassing that she has decided to live with Thomas Gerbil, the 26-year-old associate who helped me with my rule against perpetuities article."

"And?"

"And I feel terrible about all of this. I feel as if everything I've worked for through college and law school and as an associate and now as a partner in the firm is coming crashing down on me. I am beginning to wonder whether somehow I am responsible for all of this, what I might have done to make things come out differently. I even question whether the law was the right decision for me."

"Yes?"

"When I was a lad, my mom wanted me to be a doctor, and my dad wanted me to be a football star, like him. But I couldn't stand the sight of blood, so there went my medical career. And I was neither big nor fast, and I had lousy hand-eye coordination, so there went my sports career. That might not have been such a big problem, except that my adopted brother, Eugene, came along and did everything I was supposed to do. He was an all-state quarterback in high school and lettered in three sports in college. He graduated near the top of his class at Harvard

Med School, then spent ten years in Third World
countries, tending the sick under the most spartan conditions and coming to be known as the Schweitzer of the
80's, perhaps because of his accomplished organ playing.
Eugene is back in the states now, and spends his time
lecturing around the country on immunology, touring with
his organ, raising his four children (after the tragic death
of his wife, Sophia, on a mission of mercy to Sarajevo), and
polishing off the final draft of his first novel, *Life,* which
is to be published by Farrar, Straus this fall and is to be
made into a movie starring Dustin Hoffman, Barbra
Streisand, Al Pacino, Whoopi Goldberg, Bill Murray, and
Dolly Parton. All of this has me wondering whether my life
is amounting to anything."

"Uh-huh."

"Dr. Fielgud, all you've said is 'uh-huh' and 'I see' and
'yes.' Don't you have anything else to say to me?"

"Uh-huh."

"Well, what is it?"

"Your time is up. I vill see you next week. Have a
nice day."

* * *

Unfortunately, hiring Dr. Fielgud has not caused the
Fairweather firm's psychiatric problems to disappear.
Those interested in reading more about these problems
may want to watch for Dr. Fielgud's forthcoming book,
entitled *Nuts and the Law: Psychosis at Fairweather,
Winters & Sommers.*

My Last Will and Marketing Plan

by Fricka Escher

As FAIRWEATHER, Winters & Sommers' marketing director, I know that the secret to success in marketing is to make each individual attorney responsible for developing his own practice. To that end, I was able to persuade our Committee on Marketing Efforts (COME) to require each partner in the firm to adopt his or her own individual marketing plan, annually. To underline the solemnity of this undertaking, COME has required that execution of the plan conform to the formal requirements for admission of a will to probate. In order to give you an idea of just how detailed these plans have become, I've successfully armtwisted Phillip D. W. Wilson III into allowing me to print his individual marketing plan.

I, Phillip D. W. Wilson III, being of sound mind and body, hereby declare this to be my individual marketing plan for the calendar year 1995.

January

January 1. Convert annual Rose Bowl party into business development opportunity. Circulate legal pad for people in attendance to sign in. During halftime, present slide show highlighting Fairweather, Winters & Sommers services. Hand out copy of firm brochure and business card to all those in attendance.

January 2. Send warm follow-up letter to those in attendance at Rose Bowl party saying how good it was to see them, how much I value their friendship and advice, etc. Enclose another business card.

January 8. Begin campaign to become chair of the Bar Association Real Estate Subcommittee on Enfeoffment to Use and Charitable Remainder Trusts by phoning committee chair and setting up luncheon date.

January 15-19. Make follow-up calls to all of those in attendance at New Year's Day Rose Bowl party. Send follow-up letters, as appropriate, enclosing business card.

January 31. Meet with firm director of marketing to review progress in marketing plan.

February

February 1. Phone firm's partner in charge of assigning work to associates to commandeer services of two young, over-worked associates to prepare an article in my name, tentatively entitled "The Rule Against Perpetuities: Does It Still Speak to Us with Passion Today?" Explain to associates that the time they put in on this project may be billed to "non-client assignments by partners," but will be disregarded completely in compensation decisions. Assure them, however, that I will appreciate their work and will acknowledge their assistance in a footnote to the article.

February 4. Go to passport photo shop to sit for black-and-white photo to accompany article on rule against perpetuities when published in the local bar association journal. Have additional copies of photograph made for possible use in other marketing activities.

February 14. Fax valentines to everyone I've dated since third grade. Include business card.

February 20. Phone college alumni office for a complete list of the names, addresses, and phone numbers of all my college classmates.

March

March 3. Arrive at local commuter train station one half hour early. Greet commuters as they arrive, shake hands, and pass out business cards. Collect business cards from anybody who stops long enough to let me ask them for one.

March 4. Send warm follow-up letter to people who gave me business cards at train station—nice to meet you, let's do lunch sometime, if I can be of service, etc. Enclose business card.

March 10. Phone Bar Association Real Estate Committee Chair to inquire why he has not returned my call seeking to set up a luncheon date.

March 17. Wear green tie. Phone Irish friends. Follow up with letter saying it's been too long, let's hoist a few after work sometime, if I can be of service, etc. Enclose business card.

March 21. Inquire as to whether there are any local cult groups that celebrate the vernal equinox. If so, attend celebration and send follow-up letter, nice to meet you, let's do drugs sometime, if I can be of service, etc. Enclose business card.

March 31. Meet with director of marketing to monitor progress on individual marketing plan.

April

April 1. Find two partners to sponsor me for membership in the Bigwig Club.

April 3. Send Easter cards. Enclose business card.

April 10. Monitor progress of law review article being written by associates. Make sure there are an adequate number of footnotes. Submit article to bar association journal for publication, together with passport photo. Enclose business card.

April 14. Throw dinner party at home. Invite

wealthy neighbors who I have never spoken to before. Pass out business cards.

April 15. Send Passover greetings to Jewish friends. Try to get invited to a seder and make low-key business pitch while children search for matzoh.

April 23. Send warm letter to college classmates, long time no see, let's sing old college songs sometime, if I can be of service, etc. Enclose business card.

April 26. Have lunch with chairman of Bar Association Real Estate Committee. Grovel as necessary to get subcommittee chair appointment.

May

May 1. Send general mailing to everyone on my rolodex acknowledging Law Day, importance of rule of law in our society, let me know if I can be of service, etc. Enclose business card.

May 8. Send Mother's Day card to Mom, with note that it's about time for her to come in to revise her will. Enclose business card.

May 14. Contact high school alumni office to have them send list of names, addresses, and telephone numbers of all my classmates. Send warm letter to people on list, long time no see, remember the time we tore down the goal posts, if I can be of service, etc. Enclose business card.

May 25. Reorder business cards.

May 31. Meet with firm director of marketing to monitor progress on individual marketing plan.

June

June 3. Enroll in three-day course on public speaking, presentation skills, and networking.

June 14. Wear American flag lapel pin. Attend VFW luncheon. Applaud vigorously at all jingostic remarks and comment on how they don't make 'em like Patton anymore. Pass out business cards.

June 19. Send Father's Day card to Dad, with note that it's about time for him to come in to revise his will. Enclose business card.

June 24. Begin preparation of thirty-second radio ad promoting my services. Consider hiring composer to come up with catchy, but professional-sounding, jingle.

June 30. Consider whether client billable hours have dropped too drastically as a result of marketing activities.

July

July 4. Set up booth at annual Fourth of July block party to pass out free ice cream sandwiches to kids, with business cards.

July 15. Throw cocktail party at Bigwig Club to celebrate publication of "The Rule Against Perpetuities: Does It Still Speak to Us with Passion Today?" Order reprints of article to pass out with business cards. Mail copies of reprints to those unable to attend cocktail party.

July 20. Attend thirty-fifth high school reunion. Pass out copies of reprints of rule against perpetuities article, with business cards.

July 28. Air radio ad.

August

August 10. Contact grammar school office to obtain list of eighth grade classmates. Send them warm letters, long time no see, remember old Mr. Fitzmanis's nose, if I can be of service, etc. Enclose business card.

August 31. Meet with director of firm marketing to evaluate the progress of individual marketing plan.

September

September 5-6. Hold combination Labor Day/Rosh Hashanah event at Bigwig Club. Try to convince Bigwig Club to permit Jewish members.

September 30. Meet with firm director of marketing to assess progress on individual marketing plan.

October

October 10. March in annual Columbus Day parade.

October 17. Contact summer camp director for names, addresses, and phone numbers of campers who overlapped with my tenure at Camp Indianola. Write warm letter to them, long time no see, remember the old campfire stories, if I can be of service, etc. Enclose business card.

October 31. Begin building client base with trick-or-treaters by discussing their future legal needs with them. Hand out business card with miniature Milky Ways.

November

November 20. Begin work with PR agent on possible give-away program for frequent users of my legal services. Consider a free codicil for the heirs of any person whose will I've drafted who dies this year.

November 24. Try to avoid using Thanksgiving dinner to promote business, since excessive commercialism can backfire.

November 30. Meet with director of firm marketing to assess progress on individual marketing plan.

December

December 1-21. Use month to bill a few hours to clients, to nurture any existing clients who may still remain after new client development efforts for the year.

December 23. Throw cocktail party at Bigwig Club for Japanese-American friends to celebrate Emperor's birthday. Distribute reprints of rule against perpetuities article, translated into Japanese, together with business card.

December 26. Begin preparing 1996 individual marketing plan. Seriously consider leaving the firm.

*   *   *

So, as you can see, our lawyers have gotten very good at drafting impressive marketing plans. Implementing them, however, is quite another story. That may be quite fortunate for me, though. If our lawyers ever did what they said they were going to do, I would be out of a job. I'm not overly concerned about that, though.

Ex Libris?

By Samantha Priddy

WE IN THE LIBRARY fairly burst with pride when we speak of our little home. And we do regard it as that—our little home. We try to instill that same feeling in each and every one of our attorneys—partners and associates—as well. So far, we have failed miserably; but we keep on trying, because we in the library have adopted as our motto, "if at first you don't succeed, try, try again." A bit old-fashioned perhaps, but doggone it, we believe it.

Now where shall I start. There are oh-so-many things to talk about in the library . . . now if that isn't a Freudian slip: "talk in the library." Of course, a library is not a place to talk, is it. No, not at all.

Most of us can still remember when we were children going to the library and being sshed by the librarian, a gray-haired lady with wire-rimmed glasses and thick black low-heeled shoes, who wore a dark blue cardigan sweater and was called Miss Pettibone. Do you remember Miss Pettibone? Of course you do. Well, the reason Miss Pettibone sshed you was not because she was a prissy old gray-haired lady, but because the library is a place to read and study, not a place to talk.

Well, the exact same principle applies to our law library, and we on the library staff try to maintain silence, in keeping with our motto, "Silence is golden." We have tried to do this in several different ways. At strategic places around the library we posted signs that say:

NO TALKING OR WHISPERING WHATSOEVER ALLOWED
By Order of the Library Committee.

These signs achieved only modest noise-curbing success, if that; and they attracted some rather base grafitti. So we've taken them down.

We find that a more effective method is our library staff stare. When I notice two or more persons congregating and beginning to speak to one another, I dispatch one of our library staff to insert him or herself into the middle of the group and to stare silently and intently at each member of the offending group. We practice and perfect our stare techniques at library staff meetings. Unfortunately, our most effective method of enforcing silence—physical ejection from the library—has been authorized only in very limited circumstances, such as violation of the firm's strict no-ball-playing-in-the-library rule. That occurs about twice a month.

But we're not fanatics about silence, In fact, we have created a very special place in our library where talking is not only allowed, but downright encouraged—our Environmental Practice Social Room. We have named it the "Environmental Practice Social Room" because the room was made possible when our entire environmental department jumped ship to join another firm. This allowed us to jettison all of the books used by that departed department, thus making the space available to build our little social room.

Unfortunately, talking is not our only decorum problem. We have also been forced to deal with the issues of eating, smoking, and sex in the library. I'll be brief here. The former two are prohibited; the latter is permitted, but only in the Supreme Court Reporter stacks after midnight. Library users may obtain free condoms from members of CHIP, the Committee on Health in Practice. We encourage

their use since we don't want any library babies, do we. Also, "better safe than sorry," we say.

Now I don't wish to get distracted from the principal focus of our library—books. We currently house some forty-four thousand volumes on our shelves, all of them arranged according to the Stanley J. Fairweather coding system. This coding system takes into account the fact that most lawyers can remember the color of the book they want, but little else. Accordingly, we have our yellow section, our green section, our red section, our black section, and our multi-colored section. To assure specialized service to our lawyers, each of our library staff members has become expert in books of a specific color. To identify their specialties, staff members wear headbands with a feather designating their color specialties.

Our firm decorator is pushing for us to acquire more red books to lend a better balance to our library color scheme. But our library committee, mindful of the cost of acquiring new volumes, has decided instead to paint a row of black CCH Federal Tax Reporters red.

We have access to many more books through our inter-law firm book-swapping consortium, which we formed with eight of the other large law firms in town. The consortium constitution took more than six years to adopt, owing to the active and enthusiastic participation of partners from nine law firms' library committees in the negotiations. Set forth below is one of the key provisions of the constitution:

Article XI. **Book Loans**

Upon receipt of a request from a firm for a book, the Requested Firm shall promptly determine whether it owns the book and, if so, shall lend the book to the Requesting Firm unless one or more of the following conditions apply:

1. the book is in use;

2. somebody in the Requested Firm thinks he might someday use the book;

3. the Requesting Firm already has two or more books from the Requested Firm and "enough is enough;"

4. the Requesting Firm is in litigation with the Requested Firm and the book might be used effectively against the Requested Firm in such litigation;

5. the Requested Firm can't find the damn book.

Naturally, Article XI makes the swapping consortium of rather limited use to us.

One of the frustrating things for our library staff is to see so many fine books in our collection sitting there underutilized. Too often, attorneys seem to come in, pick a book off the shelf, read just one case or a few pages, and then put it back on the wrong shelf. We are attempting to expose our attorneys to the joys of exploring our library in greater depth through our newly-created Fairweather Book Circle, which selects a book each month for discussion. The title of next month's circle session is "The Use of Metaphor in Volume 52 of West's Northeastern Reporter 2nd," which promises to open new vistas in the law for former English majors.

For our younger and more hip attorneys, we are also trying to make the library more fun and user-friendly. One of our more ambitious projects is converting all of the U. S. Supreme Court cases to rap music CDs. Here are some of the lyrics to one of our most popular cases:

> *Roe v. Wade*
> *Supreme court said*
> *Keep that government*
> *Outa our bed*
> *Three trimesters*

Different rules
Justices ain't
No one's fools
Woman's body's
No-body's
But her own
Full grown
Private
Primate
Tell the state
To wait
Outside of
The gate
Stop this
Regulation dizziness
Mind their
Own business

Naturally, we fight a constant battle trying to keep track of our books. At any given time, we can generally account for 43,950 of the 44,000 books in our collection or—phrased differently—all but the 50 books that attorneys urgently need. At various times we have tried different means of encouraging attorneys to sign out books, ranging from the honor system to posting armed guards with dobermans at both exits to the library. Our current system requires attorneys to check out books using their Fairweather library card and to submit to searches of all purses and briefcases.

Another important part of our job is teaching lawyers how to use our library resources. We conduct orientation for both our summer associates and our new associates when they arrive. They seem to pay approximately as much attention to what is said at those sessions as they do to those movies of car accidents that you have to go watch when you've been given too many tickets. At least our younger attorneys, though, have some familiarity with Lexis and WestLaw research techniques. On the other hand, every time I announce that our Lexis representative has offered the firm a period of free Lexis use, several of our senior partners show up wanting to know where their car is.

In closing, I'd just like to say that this is such an exciting time to be in law libraries. The very nature of law libraries is changing almost daily. With video and audio tapes, online databases, microfiche/ultrafiche, CD-ROM and the other advances that technology is bringing, the time may not be distant when our law libraries won't need any books at all. Just think, lawyers will be able to access everything they need on-line from their own offices. This, of course, will radically reduce the amount of space we will need in the library. Come to think of it, we may not need a library at all. In fact, we may not need any staff.

So, in closing, I'd just like to say that this is a precarious and depressing time to be in law libraries. But, on the other hand, if it turns out there is no need for law libraries, then I'll finally be able to take up some of the things I've always wanted to do—like skydiving. After all, as we in the library like to say, "in every cloud there is a silver lining."

Halfalegal

by Francine Ferguson

BY THE TIME you read this, I'll be out of here. I mean like long gone.

That's not such a big surprise. I mean like paralegal is not exactly a lifelong career for a Smith College graduate, is it? No way.

Truth is, I never intended for this job to last very long. Let me tell you how I got into it in the first place.

So it's like my senior year, and me and my roommate, Muffy . . . Actually, I'm a Muffy, too. You might think that that would be confusing, two Muffies in one room. But actually, it's not. If I'm talking and I say, "Like Muffy, such and such," Muffy knows I'm talking to her. And if she's talking and says, "Like Muffy, so and so," I know she's talking to me. What would be like really confusing would be this: if you had two Muffies in one room who talked to themselves a lot . . . Anyway, me and Muffy were sitting there, doing our toes and reading Descartes, and she says to me, "Like Muffy, what are you doing next year?"

And I'm like, "How should I know, it's still *this* year."

And she's like, "I know, but people are like taking the LSATs and the GMATs and stuff, and we're like just sitting here doing our toes."

And I'm like, "No way, we're reading Descartes, too. I think and like therefore I am."

And she goes, "But Muffy, we're going to graduate in June and we've got to do something."

And I go, "Okay, okay, chill out, Muffy. We'll figure out something to do."

So she goes, "I'd really like to do something together. I mean like we're so close and everything, I'd like hate to, you know, separate."

And I go, "That's totally cool with me, so we'll just figure out something we can both do, together, okay."

And she goes, "Well, how about law school?"

And I'm like, "You gotta be kidding, Muffy."

And she's like, "No, why?"

And I go, "BOR-ing."

And she's, "How do you know that?"

And I'm like, "Because my father's a lawyer, and my brother Biff is in law school right now, and he says it's like *totally* comatose."

So she's like, "Well, maybe we should give it a try anyway."

And I'm, "No way. I'm not cashing in three of the best years I've got left for that. No way."

So she goes, "I've got it. We could be like paralegals, and see if we want to be lawyers. That doesn't take much training and you get paid really well and we can hang out with the lawyers—maybe marry one even—and carry a briefcase and I think we can get those cool embossed business cards with our names on them and . . ."

And I'm like, "Muffy, Muffy, Muffy. Okay, okay. We'll be paralegals."

So anyway, that's how I got to this position, like maybe a year and a half ago or so. And let me tell you, it's been a real eye opener. So I thought maybe I'd tell you like a little bit about it, okay?

First off, let me tell you that I'm a corporate paralegal. Muffy is a litigation paralegal with the firm. We paralegals are just about as specialized as the lawyers. You can ask Muffy about the litigation stuff. Me, I specialize in "whereases" and "now therefores." I do mainly like corporate minutes and resolutions. Fascinating stuff. And socially very important. I mean like where would we all be when the revolution comes without corporate resolutions?

Let me give you an example of the kind of thing I do. One of our clients—I'll call it xyf corporation . . . . Now that probably stops you right there, doesn't it? Lawyers call all of their corporations abc corporation or xyz corporation. If I were to do a document in which I referred to xyf corporation, I'd probably spend like half an hour talking to a partner about why I called it that instead of xyz, we'd both bill half an hour for "Conference re drafting of corporate resolution," and the client would pay.

But getting back to what I was talking about, let's like assume that xyf corporation was going to adopt a stock option plan for its officers. That resolution might go something like this:

> WHEREAS, xyf corporation has a really great group of corporate officers;
>
> WHEREAS, in order to hang on to those officers, xyf corporation must pay them at a level commensurate with the market;
>
> WHEREAS, many other corporations have stock option plans that form a major component of their compensation packages;
>
> WHEREAS, xyf corporation has no stock option plan;
>
> WHEREAS, several officers of xyf corporation have brought this fact to the attention of management;
>
> WHEREAS, management has asked its attorneys, to wit, the prestigious law firm of Fairweather, Winters & Sommers, (312) 777-7777, to whip up a really good stock option plan;
>
> WHEREAS, said prestigious law firm, to wit, Fairweather, Winters & Sommers, has drafted what they consider to be a honey of a stock option plan;
>
> WHEREAS, this board has reviewed the aforesaid

honey of a plan and concluded that adoption of said plan would be in the best interests of this corporation, its shareholders, its officers and directors, the public, and several other very important groups, too;

NOW THEREFORE, BE IT RESOLVED THAT xyf corporation shall and does hereby adopt the stock option plan attached hereto and made a part hereof as fully as if set forth herein as its very own stock option plan and does agree to honor, cherish, and obey said plan until death do it part or until said honey of a plan shall be amended or revoked, whichever shall first occur, so help xyf God.

As you can imagine, drafting resolutions like this one is like totally absorbing and gratifying. But this is not the only thing we corporate paralegals do. Not by a long shot. Here are just a few other duties of a corporate paralegal:

- We affix the corporate seal to all documents that require an embossed animal.
- We insert all minutes of corporate meetings into the appropriate corporate minute book in the exact order of the date of the meeting.
- We call the secretary of state's office to see why we never received the stamped copy of documents we filed several years ago.
- We prepare separate folders to put each of the documents needed at a closing into and label each folder.
- At closings, we help to shuffle the papers between the parties to the deal and make sure that people sign their names right next to the line on which we have put their initials.
- After closing, we put together those impressive, huge bound volumes of documents that nobody will ever look at again.
- We make sure that the corporation's articles of incorporation are put into the corporate minute books. Those articles often contain some really important provisions, like the following:

Article II. **Shareholders**

2.1 <u>Annual Meeting.</u> The annual meeting of the shareholders of abt corporation shall be held on the _____ of _____ in each year, for the purpose of lunch, electing directors, shooting the breeze a little, and for the transaction of such other business as may come before the meeting. If the day fixed for the annual meeting shall be a legal holiday, tough.

2.2 <u>Place of Meeting.</u> The board of directors may designate any place, either within or without the State of _____ (preferably someplace warm in winter), as the place of meeting for any annual meeting. If no designation is made, shareholders can call the president's secretary (phone number) who should know where it'll be.

2.3 <u>Meeting of all Shareholders.</u> If any of the shareholders shall meet at any time and place, either within or without the State of _____, such meeting shall be crowded and quite a coincidence.

2.4 <u>Closing of Transfer Books or Fixing of Record Date.</u> For the purpose of determining shareholders entitled to notice of or to vote at any meeting of shareholders, or so that it may fit in the desk, the board of directors of the corporation may provide that the stock transfer book shall be closed for a stated period, but not to exceed, in any case, sixty days, more or less. In lieu of closing the stock transfer books, the board of directors may put it in a big cabinet. The board of directors shall also have authority to repair a record date, if it is broken.

2.5 <u>Quorum.</u> A majority of the outstanding shares of the corporation, represented in person or by proxy, shall constitute a quorum at any meeting of shareholders. Ten male shareholders shall constitute a minyan. A quorum may vote, a minyan may pray and argue.

2.6 <u>Voting of Shares.</u> Each outstanding share, regardless of class or creed, shall be entitled to one vote upon each matter submitted to vote at a meeting of share-holders.

2.7 <u>Voting of Shares by Certain Holders.</u> Shares standing in the name of a deceased person may not be voted by such person. Shares standing in the name of a receiver may be voted by such receiver or by any tight end or flanker back. A shareholder whose shares are pledged is in hock, but shall be entitled to vote such shares anyway.

*   *   *

So I figure that like a year and a half of this stuff is more than enough for me. And Muffy agrees. So her and me, we're thinking about what our next step is going to be. We're like exploring our options. One possibility we're thinking about is philosophy grad school. Something that will make us like think, so we know that we are, you know. Another option we're considering is opening our own pedicure place, maybe like Muffy & Muffy's Toes, or something.

One thing for sure, though. By the time you read this, we're like out of here. And don't look for us in law school.

[WARNING: The Attorney General has determined that this chapter may be offensive to practically anyone.]

Happy Days Is Here Again

by Eileen Spindel

BEFORE I get into our travel operation at the firm, can I start with a little bit of history, about how I got this job and about travel at the firm? Good, thanks.

Now, this travel history is not by, from, and of my own personal knowledge. No, I haven't been here at the firm that long. I got this from my forebearers. Well, actually from one forebearer: Stanley.

So anyway, when I was thinking about whether to take this job, I went to Stanley and asked him how it all came about. Not that these are his words; they're not, they're mine. Except if maybe I should decide to direct quote him here and there, which you'll know from the quotation marks.

So this is maybe five, maybe six years ago we're talking about. I was a paralegal in our tax department. Anyway, it was after one of those big changes in the tax code that they do almost every year. Usually they say it's to simplify the code. Ha! Though I can't prove this (and maybe I shouldn't say it, but—what the heck—it's a free world) I think all those changes in the tax code are the work of the American Bar Association section on taxation in order to drum up more business for their members. Tax lawyers don't care *how* the tax code is changed, just so it's changed.

So I won't give you the full history of travel in the

legal profession. I mean, Stanley told me how there used
to be very little travel, since firms represented only clients
who were close to home and there wasn't much national,
and no international, business. Then he told me about how
travel was by train, because, and here I quote him, "Who
flew in those days?" But getting into the era of the
airplane—and that's the era I certainly relate to best—he
says that, until pretty recently, whenever we flew we flew
first class.

Of course, that did result in a few embarrassing
moments. Stanley told me about the time he and a young
associate were flying to Texas to close a deal on behalf of
one of the firm's large clients. They met the business guy
from the client at the gate at the airport. But when they
boarded the plane, the client went to the back and Stanley
and the associate sat up front in first-class. Stanley says
that he had the stewardess bring a drink back to the
client, on Stanley. The client wasn't all that amused.

The justifications for lawyers flying first class were
many. For one thing, it was easier to work in first class.
For another thing, it was more comfortable, less cramped
(though it's a little difficult to see how Oscar Winters,
who's five foot two, one hundred and twenty-seven pounds
dripping wet, would feel cramped in coach). Another justi-
fication was that we are first-class lawyers, so we travel
first class. The real reason, though, was that the client
paid the bill, so why the heck not travel first class, huh?

Some time after clients discovered that they didn't
have to accept, without question, the legal fees that law
firms charged them, it dawned on them that they could
question the expenses, too. This was a very unhappy day
for law firms, though nowadays it is celebrated enthusias-
tically in most parts of the world as Client Independence
Day.

So that pretty much gets us right up to the present.

You will recall that we left me as a paralegal in the tax department, which is where I was when Stanley came up to me and told me that he thought the firm needed someone to coordinate our travel, and how would I like to do it. He told me that as a tax paralegal familiar with trying to understand all of the ins and outs of the Internal Revenue Code, I would be the perfect person to make sense out of all the different airline deals and regulations. Well, one thing you learn very quickly as a paralegal (or partner) at Fairweather, Winters & Sommers is that when Stanley asks you how you would like to do something, you would like to do it very much.

Once I took over as CTO, Chief Travel Officer, my first step was to encourage our Fairweather Travel Committee to promulgate uniform travel rules for Fairweather attorneys. These rules are now embodied in the Fairweather Uniform Travel Code, and include the following:

First-class Travel. No Fairweather attorney shall travel first class on an airplane. Notwithstanding the foregoing, any Fairweather attorney may travel first class on an airplane in the following instances:

1. The client approves first-class travel in a writing witnessed by three disinterested persons at least ten days prior to the trip.

2. The attorney is using upgrade certificates purchased with his own money.

3. The flight time is over three hours and the attorney is either (a) over six foot three in his or her bare feet or (b) weighs over two hundred and thirty-five pounds and, in the judgment of CHIP, the Committee on Health in Practice, is not excessively chubby.

4. The attorney is working on highly confidential

documents, and the risk that they might be seen by a seatmate in coach is over thirty-two percent.

5. The attorney has worked more than three hundred hours on a transaction in the preceding month and is returning from closing the transaction with a certified check in excess of $500,000 in his pocket in payment of the firm's legal fees.

[EDITOR'S NOTE: Naturally, there was considerable discussion regarding these proposed new first-class travel rules, but they were adopted unanimously when Stanley threw his support in their favor with just one minor amendment. The following sentence was added to the end of paragraph 3: "Each attorney shall be deemed to be his or her own height or weight, except that Stanley J. Fairweather shall be deemed to be six foot four, two hundred and forty pounds, without an ounce of fat."]

Travel to Airports. Travel to and from airports shall be by public transportation or supershuttle wherever possible. Such travel shall be deemed impossible for members of the Executive Committee. When attorneys drive their own car to the airport, they shall use remote parking and note the location of the car on their parking ticket so as to avoid unnecessary hourly charges while searching for their car.

Drinks and Peanuts on Flights. Except for attorneys traveling first class pursuant to the first-class travel section of this Fairweather Uniform Travel Code, attorneys shall not consume alcoholic beverages at client expense while flying. Though attorneys may purchase these beverages at their own expense, CHIP warns that consumption of alcoholic beverages during pregnancy may cause birth defects. Attorneys who are traveling first class and do not wish to consume alcoholic beverages should attempt to obtain two or three of the little alcoholic drink bottles from flight attendants anyway, and return them to the firm for use at future firm cocktail parties. Similarly, all attorneys are requested to bring back any packets of peanuts that they may not consume, for use in firm conference rooms.

Overnight lodging. Wherever possible, an attorney who is traveling out of town shall attempt to avoid overnight lodging expenses through one of the following:

1. Returning to the home city on the same day as travel initiates, even if it means taking the red-eye back from California.

2. If travel is to a city in which the firm has an office, by staying at the home of a lawyer from that office.

3. By staying with a friend or relative in the destination city.

When overnight stay at a hotel cannot be avoided, Fairweather lawyers shall stay at the "Cheapest Reasonable Hotel."

"Cheapest Reasonable Hotel" shall mean, in the case of an associate who has been with the firm less than three years, Days Inn or equivalent; in the case of an associate who has been with the firm three years or more, Holiday Inn or equivalent; in the case of a partner whose client billings are less than $500,000 per year, Hilton or equivalent; and in the case of a partner whose billings are greater than $500,000 per year, Four Seasons or equivalent.

In the event that a lawyer utilizes paragraph two or three above to avoid staying at a hotel, the client shall be charged for boarding at the greater of (a) the rate of the Cheapest Reasonable Hotel or (b) the rate charged by the friend, relative, or lawyer.

Use of frequent flier miles. Frequent flier miles accumulated on client or firm travel shall be utilized to obtain free travel on client or firm trips. In the event that free travel is for travel that would otherwise be charged to

the client, the client shall be charged for the free travel at the lowest airfare available at the time.

To maximize the number of free travel awards obtained by the firm, all travel by male attorneys shall be done under the name of James Jones or Samuel Smith, and all travel by female attorneys shall be done under the name of Bonnie Black or Jane Johnson. The firm will arrange for each lawyer to obtain a James Jones, Samuel Smith, Bonnie Black, or Jane Johnson picture identification card.

Of course, as with any change at the firm, our lawyers were pretty slow to embrace this new travel policy. Some complained that our service was not "up to snuff," whatever snuff is. But, I suppose, they did have some legitimate gripes. For example, until our Computer Czar, Stevie Zwinga, came up with a computer program for us, we had one heck of a time keeping track of all our attorneys' seat preferences, special meal requests and the like. For example, there was a period of a month or two there where all of our lawyers were getting kosher meals on all their flights, which was fine with Sheldon Horvitz, but didn't make Phillip D. W. Wilson III too happy.

Recently, though, our travel services have become pretty darn popular. In fact, I just got through expanding our staff by hiring three full-time travel agents and converting a trusts and estates paralegal to a cruise director. Our new 800-number, 1-800-Stanley, makes it a lot easier for us to book vacations for our attorneys. In short, I'd say that life here at the Fairweather Happy Day Travel Agency couldn't be much better. And, as for me, I wouldn't be a tax paralegal again for anything—unless, of course, Stanley asked me if I would like to.

The Whole World in Our Hands

NOT LONG AGO the Fairweather firm hired the prestigious international consulting firm of Tellem, Wathey, Noh to report on the possibilities of the firm establishing offices abroad. Reproduced below is a portion of their report:

Introduction

With the enormous technological progress we are making in communications and transportation, the world is shrinking every day. Well, not actually, it just seems that way.

Internationalization is the byword of the nineties. To take just a small example, try sneezing. Chances are somebody is going to say, "Gesundheit." And what is Gesundheit. A German word. Internationalization. You betcha. A small example, perhaps, but telling.

And don't forget that we have a global economy. When the deutschmark goes down, you can bet that's going to affect the yen. That, in turn, of course, is going to send shockwaves through the pound, and not exactly leave the lira untouched, either. The dollar is under constant pressure now that it's floating. And you know what's happening to the price of gold. We're not sure what all of this means—and neither is anybody else—but you can bet your last pfennig that it's significant to the questions we're addressing in this report.

Should Fairweather Establish Offices Abroad?

With this as background, we can now turn to the very important question of whether Fairweather, Winters & Sommers should develop more of an international presence. As consultants, we feel constrained to point out that there are pros and cons to establishing that presence. Shall we examine them? Okay, why not.

On the one hand, if the Fairweather firm fails to develop an international presence, many other law firms will leave your firm behind in the dust. On the other hand, so what. And just what does it mean to be left behind in the dust, in any case.

Of course, establishing an international presence presents an opportunity for profit to the firm. But what are you going to do with that profit? Let's look at a hypothetical case. Suppose you set up an office in Italy and make a big profit. What are you going to get? About a gazillion lira. But it takes maybe three million lira to buy a loaf of bread, anyway. And who can tell what those funny different-sized bills mean anyway. (None of them have pictures of American presidents.) And what if the lira gets devalued? It could happen, you know. Or suppose they nationalize all law firms. Unlikely, perhaps, but not beyond the pale. And besides, let's not forget, please, that although there's an opportunity for profit, there is an even greater opportunity for loss.

Of course, there are plenty of other cogent reasons to establish an international presence, though we are having a little trouble thinking of exactly what they are right this minute. They may well have to do with the shrinking world or the global economy. But whatever they are, there are just about certainly equally or more cogent reasons not to establish that presence. So when you get right down to it, the question becomes: is there one overriding (or over-arching) reason to establish an international presence?

The answer to that one, we think, is a great big "yes." And what is that one overarching (or overriding) reason? It is the same reason that most of us put phones in our cars— it's getting downright embarrassing not to have one.

How to Establish the Office

Now that we've decided to establish a foreign office, we'd better muse a bit over just how to do it.

One way to do it is the straightforward approach of just sticking a couple lawyers on a plane, sending them over and, after a crash Berlitz course in Greenlandish, having them say, "Hi, we're Joe and Sally, it's nice to be here in Greenland. May we do your legal work?" Then you rent some space and, boom, you've got an office.

Another way of setting up an office is to acquire a foreign firm. The best way of doing that is to go to the International Foreign Firm Sale, held biannually in Bangkok, Thailand. Firms wishing to be acquired set up booths, and potential acquiring firms wander up and down the aisles checking the teeth of their prospective new partners before saying, "I think I'll take that firm over there."

The preferred way of getting a toehold internationally has become forming a strategic alliance with a foreign firm. The advantage of this approach is that it requires almost no capital; the disadvantage is that it doesn't work. While the term "strategic alliance" connotes great intrigue and stealth, most strategic alliances amount to one firm saying to another, "Hey, I've got an idea, we'll send you a little bit of business if you send us some." And the other firm replies, "Great idea, why don't we call it a strategic alliance."

What Kind of Work Should the Office Transact?

Basically, there are four types of work that you can do in your new foreign office.

1. You can represent American companies abroad. In theory this is fine, but with American firms bending over backwards to throw legal business to foreign nationals, it's not likely that this is going to generate much work.

2. Advise foreign corporations on American law. Again, fine in theory, but the problem is why do foreign corporations *care* about American law since so few of them are willing to be bound by American law anyway?

3. Advise foreign corporations on foreign law. There are two problems with this. First, you are not qualified, and second, if you tried, foreign law firms would have you thrown out of the country on your car.

4. Use your expertise on American governmental institutions and programs to represent an entire foreign country, set up their constitution, legal system, regulatory laws, etc. This will provide an extremely useful service to the foreign country, since it will permit them to achieve almost overnight the same mess that it has taken our country centuries to accomplish. Of course, the long-term problem with this type of representation is that there are only a limited number of foreign countries to go around. Come to think of it though, with the recent radical changes in the world and the split-up of countries, that limitation may not prove to be such a big problem, after all.

Where to Set Up Your Office

In helping you to determine where to set up your foreign office or offices, we have identified the following eleven questions for you to ask yourself:

1. Is this a very dangerous country, in which many

of my new partners and associates are likely to be exterminated?

2. What's the weather like?
3. How is the economy of this country? Do we see pictures of very thin people on the front page of the newspaper, fat sleazy-looking people shaking our president's hand in *Newsweek*, or naked people in *National Geographic*?
4. Is the government of this country friendly to the United States, or are our partners likely to become hostages?
5. How's the shopping?
6. Is there strong competition in this country's legal community?
7. Can anybody in our firm speak the language of this country?
8. Does Baker & McKenzie already have an office there?
9. Is the food too spicy?
10. Has anybody at our firm ever heard of this country?
11. What are the chances that this country will be in existence two years from now?

Of course, many of these factors lead to conflicting conclusions as to whether you should establish an office in a particular country. Therefore, to give a more impartial view of the subject, we tried this experiment. First we placed a large map of the world on the wall of a conference room at our office. Then we blindfolded Stinky Frommer, one of our brightest new consultants, spun him around, and asked him to throw a dart at the wall. This method suggests that you should open an office in the northeastern quadrant of the Indian Ocean.

Conclusion

The opening of international offices offers significant opportunities, but also creates serious problems. On the positive side, it is difficult for any major law firm to be taken seriously today without a major international presence. On the other hand, opening a number of international offices poses significant economic risks that we could not advise you to undertake, especially given what we know from our recent review of your current financial status. We therefore suggest that in order to create the prestige and aura of an international law firm, without the attendant economic drain, you add Bombay, Hong Kong, London, Paris, Prague, Sidney, and Tokyo to your letterhead—but that you not open new offices in any of these cities.

Sweet Dreams

by Elizabeth Monarch

WORKING on the night staff at Fairweather, Winters & Sommers reminds me a little of my first scuba dive at night.

When I jumped into the water, it was pitch black, very disorienting; in fact, I had trouble figuring out which way was up. Once I got my bearings, though, I discovered a whole new world down there. Working on the Fairweather night staff is a lot like that. You have to get used to thinking of the day starting at 6 P.M. and ending at 6 A.M. It's a bit disorienting at first, but rather delightful, really—once you figure out which way is up.

Like many of our other night staffers, I started out at the firm working days, as a secretary. But after my first kid, Stanley, was born, I quit. A few months later, I got a call from our secretarial supervisor, Cathy Grosuede, asking if I'd like to come in nights. When I said I'd give it a try, I became the first full-time night staffer. Up until then, it had been pretty much catch as catch can, trying to get the firm's work done over night by asking day secretaries late each afternoon if they could stay around to work that evening.

Once I started coming in and working evenings regularly, lawyers started to like the idea that they could rely on somebody being there, so a few additional night secretaries were hired. That remained the situation for at least a year, until one day it dawned upon one of the financial geniuses on our Executive Committee, who at the time was reading a history of the industrial revolution, that the firm owned all these lawyer-machines that they were paying fixed salaries to. If the firm could keep those machines running all night, billable hours and therefore profits would soar. Against this extra revenue, the additional cost of the support staff necessary to produce that work was peanuts. (In fact, somebody eventually figured out that the firm could charge clients separately for night support staff, and make a profit on that, too.)

So pretty soon, the firm had developed a full night staff—word processing, photocopying, etc. And because of my extraordinary qualifications for the job—I happened to have been the first night staffer—I was made manager of them all, Queen of the Night.

I soon learned that providing the support staff necessary to get the work produced was the easy part of my job. The lawyers who stayed down late figured that they were entitled to some fringe benefits for staying down and, as Queen of the Night, I was responsible for figuring out how to satisfy those demands. That took some creativity. To give you some idea of just how much progress we've made, I taped a discussion in which Fred Lieber and Joy Waxel, two of our regular night-owl lawyers, and Larry Niz, who was staying late for the first time, discuss working at night.

Larry: Mind if I ask you a few questions?

Fred: Hey, no problem, we've got lots of time. It's only eight now, and we've got until nine tomorrow morning.

Joy: Yes, that's one of the things we like about working nights: no big rush to get things done in the next hour or two. When else in the practice do you get twelve or fifteen hours to respond these days? What's on your mind?

Larry: Well, I was getting a little hungry. What do you do for dinner, hit the vending machines? Order some pizza in?

Joy: Heck, no. That's what we've got a chef for. Dinner is served in the conference room on 77 North, or Chez Fairweather, as we call it.

Fred: Yes, I think the main course choices for tonight are veal cordon bleu and halibut steak in a white wine sauce, if I'm not mistaken.

Larry: Pretty nice, but I suppose I'm too late for that.

Joy: No, there are two seatings each evening, 7:30 and 9:30. You may want to call over to Jean-Louis, the maître d', though, to try to reserve a table by the window.

Larry: Table by the window? But there's just one large rectangular conference table in there.

Fred: During the day, yes. But at night that table is moved out and small tables with blue-checkered tablecloths and silver candlesticks are moved in.

Larry: Sounds very fancy.

Joy: Oh, it is. The photographs of the firm's founders come down and French posters go up. The place is really transformed.

Fred: And the view over the city is quite spectacular from the window tables. In fact, I'll call over and have Jean-Louis set another place at our table tonight, so you'll be sure to have the view.

Larry: Oh, I hate to barge in like that.

Joy: It's no problem at all, we'd love to have you.

Larry: Well, thank you very much, then. This type of dinner must be quite expensive for the firm.

Fred: The prix fixe is $85, plus wine and tip, of course. So you don't want to eat there unless you're staying down on client work and can bill the dinner to the client.

Larry: Hey, am I seeing things, or was that Kathy Ruscant who just walked by in slippers and a white robe with FW&S embroidered in maroon?

Joy: No, you're right, that was Kathy. I think she's in Steve Falderall's office for the night.

Larry: She's sleeping on the couch in there?

Joy: Oh, heavens no. Our night moving crew moves all of the furniture out of the corner offices for the evening, and sets them up with king-sized beds, TV, minibar, the works.

Larry: But don't the senior partners object to having their offices used like that?

Fred: Most of them don't even know about it. They're never here past 6:30, and by the time they get in the next morning, everything is set up just the way they left it the day before. And those who do know about it don't object anyway, since it's turned into quite a significant revenue source for the firm.

Larry: You mean we charge clients hotel rates for the use of the rooms?

Joy: Of course we charge them. Why wouldn't the Omni-Fairweather charge?

Larry: We're an Omni? What do rooms go for?

Joy: I'm not sure what the rate is, it changes quite often. Depends on the season, and whether there's a big convention in town. Of course we offer special weekend packages. If you're curious, you could call our night receptionist, who also serves as the front desk clerk. But if you're planning to stay the night, you really ought to book a room now. Turn down service is only available until 10:30, and if you miss that, no chocolates on your pillow.

Larry: Chocolates on your pillow? Are you kidding? What else is available?

Fred: To get the full story, you really should call Herman,

our concierge. He used to work at the Four Seasons across the street, 'til we lured him away. I can tell you, though, that there's a complimentary shoe shine if you leave your shoes in a bag on the door knob before 2 A.M., room service available 24 hours, and I think you get 500 frequent flier miles on United for each night you stay.

Larry: This is amazing. I had no idea all of this existed at the firm. What do lawyers who stay late do to kill time if there are breaks in their work, like while you're waiting for word processing to produce a revised draft of a document?

Joy: There are quite a number of options, actually. Of course, if you are staying the night, you can always choose to watch TV in your room. But if you don't want to do that, there is a feature-length film in 77 South conference room every night, and 76 North is converted to a game and card room. In 76 South, we have live entertainment—tonight I think it's a folk singer—and dancing from 10 P.M. 'til 3.

Larry: This is great. I'm going to switch my hours and become a night owl myself.

Fred: I'm afraid that's not going to be possible. You see, everybody who finds out about what goes on here at night has that reaction, so we've had to limit the number of people who can stay down each evening. Otherwise we'd have trouble filling our offices during the day. Besides, we're getting a lot of complaints.

Larry: What's that? Complaints from whom?

Joy: Well, you know, relationships tend to form down here.

Larry: What do you mean by that?

Fred: Well, Joy and I got married six months ago.

Larry: That's wonderful, congratulations.

Joy: Thanks a lot, but our former spouses aren't too happy about it. They've threatened to sue the firm for alienation of affections.

Larry: I see. You do spend a lot of time down here.

Fred: Oh yes, we're residents. We have adjoining offices and reserve Phillip Wilson's corner office, next door, each night, so it would be silly to pay rent somewhere.

Joy: Yes, and we figure that by the time we're ready to have kids we'll both be partners, with nice, large, adjoining partner-sized offices and we'll just knock down the wall between us, make a nice little play area for junior, and . . .

So, as you can see, we've become a little too successful making our lawyers feel comfortable around this place at night. There's a sense of camaraderie and fun that doesn't exist during the day anymore. Things move a bit slower, people are a bit friendlier . . . it's all rather delightful, really, once you figure out which way is up.

Benefits with a Doubt

by Babette Footbury

EVERYTHING'S *so* complicated. You wouldn't believe it. Why, I don't know. But knowing is not my job. You know how it is, "yours is not to reason why, yours is but to do or die."

Dying, by the way, is one of them. The benefits we provide. No, wait a minute, that sounds funny. *Dying* is not the benefit, *life insurance* is. We provide life insurance because although I think it was Edna St. Vincent Millay who said, "Life goes on forever, like the gnawing of a mouse," we at the Fairweather firm have not found that to be true (the going on forever part, I mean, not the gnawing mouse).

But maybe I should back up. I'm in charge of benefits here at Fairweather, Winters & Sommers. And do we have benefits! Up the wazoo, you'll pardon the expression, we have benefits. We have health insurance, we have life insurance, supplemental life insurance we have, travel accident insurance, long-term disability, medium-term disability, very short disability, profit sharing, loss sharing, vacations, a cafeteria plan, not to mention the cafeteria itself, and child care. I'll tell you, it's a full-time job keeping up with it all. Come to think of it, that's why they hired me: to keep up with it all.

Now, I'm not going to try to tell you about everything. Heavens no. We have about twenty-six pounds of printed material that we give to people to describe all of that. No, I'll just pick out a few highlights.

Let's talk insurance, okay? Now if you try to read the actual insurance policies themselves, you would find them impossible to understand. That's probably why nobody tries to read them. In fact, no one understands insurance policies, including the people who draft them. Fortunately, though, it's easy enough to grasp the basics, so I'll give them to you here: our lawyers' coverage for the big two— life and health.

Life. The firm pays premiums for life insurance for attorneys. The amount of insurance we provided used to be equal to two-and-a-half times an attorney's income for the prior year. The effect of this, of course, was to provide greater insurance benefits to attorneys with larger incomes, who therefore presumably needed those benefits less.

When the firm realized this effect, we approached our insurance carrier and made the sensible proposal that the firm list all attorneys in order of their salary and that the attorney with the lowest salary be insured in an amount equal to two-and-a-half times the amount of the salary of the highest person and vice versa, all the way up and down the list. The firm pointed out that the total amount of insurance written would be the same and that the likely amount of payout by the insurance company would probably be even less, since the people with the lowest salaries and therefore the highest insurance would tend to be younger and so less likely to die.

Our insurance carrier refused to agree to this, how- ever. They argued that the high insurance benefits would give our younger attorneys too much incentive to die quickly and that attorneys were well known to be willing to do anything to make a quick buck, especially if it would screw an insurance company.

To combat the insurance company's intransigence,

however, our firm decided to have the person with the highest salary name the person with the lowest salary as beneficiary of his insurance policy and vice versa. While this did not accomplish the purpose of life insurance, since benefits were payable on somebody else's death, it did seem like a clever ploy and so we tried it.

When the insurance company got wind of this trick, however, it adopted a requirement that the beneficiary of each of our attorney's insurance policies be related to the insured. Undaunted by that technical requirement, though, our firm arranged for each older insured to legally adopt his or her beneficiary. (This required modifying the firms' no nepotism rule, but we pushed that amendment through the Executive Committee in a matter of only a few months.) The firm was pleased at having outwitted the insurance company until we received notice from our insurer that it was canceling the firm's policy.

We have now found a new insurer. The bad news is that we've had to agree to go back to the old formula for benefits. But the good news is that if one of our lawyers is clever enough to die on a business trip, his beneficiaries collect double.

Health. The idea behind our health insurance is easy—if you get sick or injured, hey, don't worry about it, our health insurance company is going to take care of everything. Naturally, there are a few simple wrinkles you should be aware of.

If you have a pre-existing condition, then, of course, our health insurance is not going to pay for anything caused by that. After all, it's not their fault if you had the sniffles as a kid and so are susceptible to pneumonia now, is it?

And they're going to want to make sure that the expenses you incur are really necessary. That stands to reason. For example, it's become so trendy these days for lawyers to have quadruple bypass surgery that everyone thirty-five and older can't wait to have one so that they can flash their scars at the health club (membership in which is another firm benefit, by the way—for partners only, of course).

To protect against those unscrupulous partners who would be running in to have their quadruple bypasses whether or not they needed them, our insurance company requires that you obtain at least six opinions that any operation you are about to have is necessary, and to wait four months before having it. Inevitably this means that a certain number of our fine lawyers will die before the operation can be performed. But then that's one of the reasons we have *life* insurance, isn't it?

Of course, our insurance company is not about to just write a blank check, pay whatever those greedy doctors think something's worth. Through experience, our insurance company has been able to pinpoint just how much a lawyer's organs are worth. So if a lawyer loses an eye, it's good for fifty grand. Lose both eyes, though, and they'll pay not one hundred, but two hundred thousand dollars. A lawyer's fingers are not worth all that much, so you might as well hang onto them. But if you're willing to give up an arm—and, frankly, arms are not all that important to what lawyers do—well, that would really be worth your while.

To contain soaring medical costs, the firm has modified coverage slightly in recent years. First off, since hiring our firm psychiatrist, Dr. Helpem Fielgud, we have excluded mental health coverage. Second, since most of our partners and their spouses are no longer fecund (and excessive hours has snuffed out the sex drives of many others), we have eliminated pregnancy coverage. Third, to avoid the firm footing the bill for spouses in marriages doomed to fail, spouse coverage starts only after the tenth wedding anniversary, and premiums paid by the firm for spouses must be reimbursed by lawyers in the event of divorce. Fourth, our deductible has been increased from $100 to 10% of the lawyer's annual salary. And finally, the firm has taken another important step in reducing the cost of our health insurance: instead of relying on high-priced specialists, our current plan calls for all services to be provided by third-year medical students in the bottom half of their class at the local medical school.

That's not ideal, I know, but at least any mistakes the med students make are covered by our insurance (if, of course, you get the six medical opinions that say that the corrective procedure is necessary.)

To compensate for our cost-saving cutbacks, we have negotiated a special category of lawyer-diseases for which the firm provides full coverage. To give you some idea of what's included in this category: heart attacks during or within ten minutes after the end of any partnership meeting, loss of sight that's shown to be attributable to reading small print in adhesion contracts, injuries sustained through intentional acts of clients after receiving fee statements or news of unfavorable jury verdicts in excess of two million dollars, and disability due to terminal boredom. (By the way, the firm looked into purchasing a general disability policy for our lawyers, but the insurance company declined coverage when their analysis showed that over sixty percent of our partners already were disabled, one way or another.)

We have also investigated allowing our attorneys to establish flexible spending accounts for medical expenses that permit up to $3000 of those expenses to be paid on a pre-tax basis. The requirements for qualification for these deductions, however, have proved too complex for our ERISA department to understand. In lieu of establishing those accounts, therefore, the Executive Committee has decided simply not to report $3000 of each attorney's income to the Internal Revenue Service. While this decision presents obvious legal risks, the Executive Committee knows that our tax department is not very busy anyway and an IRS challenge would give them some good practice.

* * *

So that gives you a quick look-see at just a couple of our benefits. If you'd like to see more, you can come over and take a look at the twenty-six pounds of printed material that describes it all. But I should warn you—the last person who decided to do that threw his back out trying to lift it. And so far, our insurance company's denying coverage.

Hello There,
Is Anybody Home?

by Virginia Strately

FOR MANY LAWYERS, especially partners, the telephone has become an extremely intimidating instrument. Most partners made the adjustment from a rotary dial to touchtone with only a modicum of difficulty (although, if you watch closely, you'll notice that senior partners still touch the numbers on their phone with a circular motion). But when it got beyond that, the vast majority of partners got lost. About the time telephones started getting really complicated, our entire environmental law department upped and went to another firm. That left me, as our sole environmental law paralegal, with a little free time on my hands. So the firm made me its first director of telephone services.

At first I spent a lot of my time holding the hands of older partners, and placing calls for them. As they became more accustomed to our new phones, however, I started to devote most of my time to developing a gripping new telephone manual, entitled *Your Telephone, Your Friend*. Now, of course, most every law firm has a manual with technical descriptions of how to operate the telephone system and voice mail. But only *Your Telephone, Your Friend* provides both technical advice and helpful hints as to just *why* one might want to use the features of the system. Here is an excerpt from that manual.

Call forward. This feature allows you to take your phone calls at another number. Thus, for example, if you are going to be in a conference room and are expecting an important call, you may forward your calls to the conference room. Your important call will not come through while you are in the meeting. However, you will be able to field telephone calls from partners who have used that conference room for the last two weeks, forwarded their calls there, and forgotten to unforward them afterwards. The next day, when you are back in your own office, your important call will go to the conference room. If you ever want to receive another phone call in your office, it is best not to use this feature. Ever.

Call park. This feature allows you to pick up a call at one telephone and retrieve it at another extension. By following the simple eight-step procedure, you can accomplish essentially the same thing as you can by pressing the hold button.

Conference. This feature theoretically allows you to bring a third party at another extension into your phone call. In fact, what it allows you to do is to disconnect people so that they don't think you hung up on them intentionally. This is a very useful feature when you have received a phone call from somebody to whom you do not want to speak or are not yet prepared to speak. Simply tell them, "Hang on, I'm going to hook Joe into this call." Then follow the conferencing procedure, which will disconnect everybody. When the person calls you right back, you can have your secretary answer the phone and say that you have been called out to an important meeting, but will call that person back in a month or two.

Directory. This feature allows you to enter the names and phone numbers of up to one million clients, potential clients, friends, relatives, and service providers. By spelling out the person's name and pressing the correct button, you can dial this person "automatically." This time-saving device really takes about twice as long as it would take you to look up the person in your Rolodex and dial the number yourself.

Hold. This feature allows you to test how important you are to your callers, by putting them on hold. When combined with the automatic timer feature on the phone, this will measure the length of time the person who has called you is willing to wait before hanging up. The firm record is held by Stanley Fairweather, who once went on a two-week vacation and returned to pick up the phone and find that the associate to whom he had been speaking was still on the line.

Long-distance charging. This feature allows you to code in the client's telephone number, the firm-client number, the client's date of birth and wedding anniversary date, then dial a wrong number and automatically bill it to the client.

Message. This feature, when lit, indicates that there is a message for you in your voice mail. Ignore it; if it's important enough they'll call back.

Message waiting. This feature, when lit, indicates that the receptionist has a package or person waiting for you in the reception area. If not claimed in two weeks, the package or person will be returned.

Musak. This feature allows you to select music of your choice for the caller to listen to while he or she is waiting to be disconnected by you.

Mute. This feature allows you to speak to another person in your office while a phone conversation is going on, without allowing the person on the other end to hear your conversation—usually. It was the malfunctioning of this feature that cost the firm one of its largest clients when he overheard a partner telling some associates,

"Don't worry about old Fred, he's just blowing off steam. Really he's a pussycat."

Redial. This feature allows you to mistakenly call the person you have just hung up with, instead of the person you spoke to only a minute before, whom you thought was the last person you spoke to.

Room service. If you have this feature on your phone, you have checked into the Four Seasons Hotel across the street from our office. Please call the receptionist on your floor at the firm for directions as to how to return to your office.

Send calls. This feature allows you to send calls directly to your secretary or voice mail. You will hear a little ping tone as calls come in, thus making you so curious that you will immediately phone your secretary or access your voice mail messages to see who has just called, thus defeating the entire purpose of the send calls feature.

Signal. This feature, when pressed, buzzes at your secretary's desk, scaring the hell out of your secretary and indicating that either (a) you wish to speak to your secretary on the intercom, (b) you wish your secretary to come into the office, or (c) more likely, you have hit the signal button in error.

Speaker. This feature permits you to affect the appearance that you have been reached in a cave. It also allows you to keep both hands free to play with your waste basketball set or to eat brunch while talking on the phone. Associates are not issued speaker phones since if they had them there would be nothing left to which to aspire in attaining partnership.

Speed calls. This feature allows you to reach another number by pressing only two or three keys, instead of dialing the full telephone number. You will want to code in your barber or beautician, your health club, your dry cleaners and, perhaps, a client or two. CAUTION: Do

NOT code in your home telephone number. A discrete mechanism in the telephone causes you to forget immediately any number that you have coded in. It becomes extremely embarrassing when somebody asks you for your home number and you are forced to reply *13. Ditto for illicit lovers. A fun game for associates is to go around to partners' offices after 5 o'clock—when they all will have left for the day—and dial the partner's speed numbers to find out whom they have coded in.

Timer. This feature allows you to calculate exactly how long you have spoken to a client, for purposes of billing. Those accustomed to billing a quarter hour for a four-minute conversation may disregard the timer feature. The timer is also useful in allowing you to calculate the amount of time it takes you to run around your floor. To stimulate greater use of the timer for billing, the firm is in the process of developing a taximeter feature which will encourage the attorney to push down the flag at the beginning of a conversation, and the billable amount will automatically increase each minute as the conversation progresses. The attorney will be able to toggle the "extras" button on the meter when he or she gives particularly sage advice.

Transfer. This feature allows you to shift your call to another lawyer in the firm. It is particularly useful to senior partners in shifting responsibility and blame downward for matters that they should have handled themselves. The transfer feature may also be used as a substitute for the conference call function to disconnect all parties.

Wake up. This feature allows senior partners to request the receptionist to rouse them from their mid-afternoon nap at a predetermined hour.

VOICE MAIL FEATURES

Security. Each voice mail user has the ability to enter a password that will allow only that person to access his or her voice mail messages. Unfortunately, the firm has experienced a spate of instances in which partners have forgotten their passwords, thereby making weeks of messages irretrievably unretrievable. To combat this problem, the firm has hired a Director of Password Recollection with whom all attorneys must register their password.

Broadcast. This feature allows you to send the same message to everyone in the office or to a selected group of people. Primary use for this feature is to try to scalp your tickets to a sporting or artistic event to others at the firm at the last minute.

Personal greeting. This feature allows you to record or change the personal greeting in your voice mail. The firm recommends the following, "Press the # key to skip this greeting."

Extended absence greeting. This feature allows you to record a message to your callers when you will be away from the office for a period of time. The firm recommends the following wording, "Oh hi, this is _____. I'm finally getting out of here on vacation. Me and my spouse are going on a well-deserved trip to France for three weeks. Feel free to leave a message, but don't expect me to get back to you. If you need immediate help, press 0 and pray. Have a bon jour."

* * *

Of course, *Your Telephone, Your Friend* has not been our only project at telephone services. Only recently, for example, we developed the following message that will play when our telephone arteries are clogged with calls:

We're sorry, all of our lawyers and paralegals are busy assisting other clients right now. Please hold; your call will be answered in the order it was received. For pour-over wills with contingent remainder trusts, press 1; for temporary restraining orders, press 2; for quick answers to complicated legal questions, press 3 . . .

Rest assured that we in telephone services anxiously await the next advances in communication, whatever they may be. We've no doubt that those advances will help us to live up to our motto: "Making your life more complicated through technology."

Bon Appetit

by Chef Pierre Effete

Bᴏɴ ᴊᴏᴜʀ. Mon name ees Pierre Effete. I am zee chef at zee Fairweather firm, since a few years ago. Prior to zat, I am zee chef at a Michelin two-star restaurant in zee south of France, near Provence. My restaurant zere ees called La Queue du Cochon. Which mean "Tail of zee Pig." It is a stupid name, I know. But nobody cares about zat because zee food, it ees very good.

You may ask me, "Chef Pierre, how come you leave a fine restaurant in zee south of France to become zee chef at zee Fairweather firm?" Many days, I ask myself zis same question, why I leave. Zee answer to zat question, though, ees Stanley Fairweather.

Five or six years ago, I theenk, I don't know which, Mr. Fairweather come to my restaurant. We talk. I find out zat he ees a chef himself. We talk about zee dinner I prepare, and I see zat he knows very much about zee food and zee preparation. Also, he knows very much about zee wines in my restaurant. I am very impressed, because most of zee Americans who come into my restaurant, zay know nuzzing about what zay are eating or drinking, only zay know zat zay should love it very much. Why is zis zay should love it? Because Mr. Michelin, he tell zem to.

Zee next night, Mr. Fairweather come back to my restaurant and we talk again. He come back into my kitchen and I explain to him zee preparation of zee food. He talk with me about some dishes zat he prepare back home and he write me down zee recipe for a deesh he call

Cheeken Stanley. He also talk to me about how he want to improve zee food service at heez firm, to make it somezing really especiale.

Zee next night, Mr. Fairweather he come back again to my restaurant. Again we talk, and again he talk to me about how I could make zee food service at his firm somezing really especiale, and how I should come back to Chicago with heem.

Pretty soon, I don't know why, I'm telling my owner from my restaurant zat I am leaving zee restaurant, I'm going back to Chicago with Mr. Fairweather. My owner from my restaurant tell me zat I am out of my mind completely, and zat he does not want such a crazy cook around his restaurant, anyway; zat now maybe he will get zee third star.

In zees way, I am coming to be zee chef at zee Fairweather firm.

For me, zee change in my life has, how do you call it, zee ups and zee downs. At first, it has for me almost always zee downs.

To me, zee first zing a fine food service department must have eez a fine wine list. I am very surprised to find out zat zee Fairweather firm does not serve wine with zee meals. So I go talk with Mr. Fairweather about zis.

He explain to me about zee dram shop laws. He explain to me zat this mean zat if somebody get, how you say it, schnockered from too much wine and crash and hurt somebody with hees car, zee firm is responsible for zis. Zis I do not understand. In France we do not have zee dram shop.

But it ees very important to me zat I have zee wine, dram shop or no dram shop, I tell Mr. Fairweather. So Mr. Fairweather he decide to form zee Fairweather Committee on Wine, which zay call COW. Zis committee it meet many times, very many times, about zee dram shop problem.

Finally, after maybe six or seven meetings, COW decide
zis—zat zay can't decide nuzzing. Rather, zay must talk to
zee Fairweather Insurance Committeee about getting zee
coverage for zee dram shop liability. Zis is a down for me.

Zee Insurance Committee takes many months to
discuss zis question. Like zee COWs, zay also have many
questions, but no many answers. From who should zay buy
zis coverage? How much coverage should zay buy? Should
it cover zee hard liquor in addition to zee wine? And how
much will zis insurance cost? About zis last question, zay
decide zay must talk to zee Finance Committee. Zis is
another one of my downs.

Zee Finance Committee also meets many times. Zay
consider zee size of zee deductible, zee stability of zee
insurance companies, payments by zee month or by zee
quarter. Zay consider everything and finally zay decide zat
since zee insurance will cost more zan one hundred dollars
per year, zay must talk to zee Executive Committee. Zis is
another down for me.

Now zee Executive Committee meet about zee same
thing zat zee COWs and zee Insurance Committee and zee
Finance Committee meet about. Finally, at zee third
meeting of zee Executive Committee to discuss zis
question, Mr. Fairweather says zat he brought me to zee
firm all zee way from France and zat zere will be wine at
zee firm. Zis is one of my ups.

Next, I am surprised when zee COWs want to meet
with me again. I am thinking that we have decided about
having zee wine and we do not need to meet again, zat I
am through with zee COWs. But zee COWs think udder
wise. Zis time zee COWs want to talk about which wines
we drink. One of zee COWs, Sheldon Horvitz, want to
select a wine zat I have not heard of before, zee Mogen
David, so I have to taste zee Mogen David, kosher for
Passover. And, he say, when we use zis wine, we have to

say zee bracha. So I have to buy zee Mogen David, kosher for Passover, and learn zee bracha. But finally, zee COWs and me, we decide on all zee wines. Zis is one of my ups.

So now zat we solve zee wine problem, I turn to zee food. Here we have even more problems than with zee wine.

First thing I find out is zat zee Fairweather lawyers no like my goose liver pâté. I tell zem zat it win zee Prix de Paris for zee best hors d'oeuvre in 1986. But zis does not matter to zee partners. So I say, okay, if you don't like zee goose liver pâté, I make you zee duck foie gras. But zee partners say zay prefer zee Pringles potato chips with zee onion dip instead. Zis is for me another down.

Next thing I find out we have no stove to cook on. Zee building requirements prevent having zis. So I go to Stanley. "Zis is worse zan zee dram shop," I say. But he tells me, "Relax, Pierre, you have zee meecrowave."

But naturally, zis limits my cooking range, zee meecrowave. Zis means I must cook zee meals someplace else and zen, how you say it—zap zee suckers in zee meecrowave. I find zat zis does not work out very well, zere is a reason we do not use zee meecrowave in zee two-star restaurants in France. Besides, it is very expensive because we have to rent a place outside zee firm for me to cook and zen send zee meal by limo to zee firm. Zis does not fit within my prix fixe.

So finally I ask zee partners, "Okay, what did you do before I arrive." And zay tell me zat zay order from zee Mahzel Deli. Fine, I think, if zay want zee sanwich, I can fix zem zee sanwich. So, I make zee sanwich. And zay are deleeshus, I say myself.

But, of course, zis means zat we are ordering very little food from zee Mahzel Deli. And zee Mahzel Deli is a client of zee firm. So zee Mahzel Deli complain to zee firm. At zee same time, zee waiters and zee waitresses I have hired to deliver zee sandwich, zay are coming to me and zay are threatening to quit because of zee small tips zay get from zee lawyers at zee firm. Zis, for me, is another big down.

Finally, I go to Stanley and I tell heem everything. I complain to him zat he make me leave my restaurant in Provence for zis, and zat I am going back home. But he say to me, "Pierre, why you no come to me before zis?"

And Stanley sit down and he make a plan. He say to me, "Pierre, we are doing zis. Zee Fairweather firm, we will buy zee Mahzel Deli and zen we are changing it to zee finest French restaurant in zee city. In zis new restaurant," he say, "Pierre will cook zee meal zat he chooses and also Pierre will pick zee wines. From zis restaurant, we will also serve zee public." Mr. Fairweather also say to me zat zis will be a big profit center to zee firm (what zis profit center means I do not know, but I think it is very good). And zee name of zee new restaurant it will be, "Stanley and Pierre's Tail of zee Pig."

Zis, for me, is a big up.

Exhausted Remedies

[The editors are grateful to the Harvard, Yale, and Stanford Law Reviews, in which the following article appeared simultaneously, for permission to excerpt the article here. The article also appeared, without footnotes, in *Rolling Stone*.]

Resolving Intra-Firm Disputes Peaceably: Laundering Your Own Suits

by Nails Nuttree*

We live in a litigious society[1] (and, as a prominent litigator myself,[2] I might add, thank heavens we do). To give you some historical perspective, our system of government is based on the rule of law[3] and descends from really old-time documents, like the Magna Carta and the Code of Hamurabi.[4] Probably the Greeks and Romans had something to do with it, too, since they seem to have had something to do with practically everything.

In recent years, people, notably clients, have noticed the high cost of litigation.[5] This has led to pressure to develop less expensive ways of resolving disputes. A couple of the more popular ways that have been developed are flipping a coin and splitting the difference.

These changes in dispute resolution threaten to rend the very fabric of our legal system and, more importantly, to cut drastically into the profits of large law firms. Fortunately, however, law firms have proved equal to the challenge, reacting quickly to provide vital new legal services to clients in these areas, with a view towards making these simple dispute resolution techniques as complex and expensive as litigation. Our firm, for example, has just created a sub-group within the litigation department (which department the author of this article proudly chairs) on flipping-the-coin law.[6]

I've gotten a bit off the topic of this article, which is on resolving intra-firm disputes, but not by much. The point is, not even we law firms have been immune to the horror of litigation. Some employees of our firms, ingrates that they are, have taken it upon themselves to sue us— and that after all we've done for them.

And we law firms, of all people, must be aware of the high cost of litigation, having created it ourselves. To stem that cost at Fairweather, Winters & Sommers, we have required all of our employees to sign a simple agreement that requires them to resolve any disputes they may have with our firm through FADS, the Fairweather Alternative Dispute System.

The complete rules and regulations of FADS comprise one hundred sixty-three pages and so are far too voluminous to reproduce here.[7] Instead, I will set forth a few of the key elements of those rules:

1. Potential complainants (referred to as "Ingrates" in the FADS code) are required to exhaust all possible administrative remedies, no matter how futile, prior to instituting a FADS action. These administrative remedies include talking to the Ingrate's supervisor; talking to the Ingrate's supervisor again; going to the appropriate firm committee, if any; going to the inappropriate firm committee; talking to the Ingrate's supervisor yet again; and waiting three months to see if the Ingrate doesn't feel a little better after letting it all settle down for awhile.

2. Ingrates are permitted to be represented by counsel, except that no member of the firm may represent

an Ingrate, because of potential conflicts of interest, unless the Ingrate is able to pay our hourly rates, thinks that the potential conflict is no big deal, and signs the firm's conflict waiver form.

3. In order to prevail, an Ingrate must establish his/her case by a 65% preponderance of the evidence.

4. If an Ingrate prevails, the case is presented two more times to two different judges and the best two out of three wins.[8]

5. If an Ingrate wins two out of three, the firm may elect to go double or nothing by flipping a coin and, if the coin comes up heads, the firm wins.

6. If the Ingrate prevails on the first coin flip, then there shall be two more flips, and the best two out of three wins.[9]

7. In case of a hung jury, something's gone wrong, since there is no jury trial under FADS.

8. All proceedings take place in the Fairweather Moot Court Room and are presided over by retired state court judges who are paid by the firm.

While it is early in our firm's history with FADS, and the jury is still out,[10] initial results looks encouraging. The following table shows the results to date, in the year that FADS has been in effect:

Cases still in "exhausting the remedies" stage	243
Cases firm won first time around	2
Cases firm won, best two out of three	3
Cases firm won, initial coin toss	19
Cases firm won, best two out of three coin tosses	15
Cases firm lost	1

It's clear that we law firms must adjust to the new litigious society and that establishing an intra-firm dispute resolution system is an important step in that direction. It is the hope of the author that this article may stimulate creative thought in this area. Should you wish additional information about setting up an intra-firm dispute resolution system, feel free to call the intra-firm dispute resolution sub-group of our litigation department.

While the need for these types of dispute resolution systems may sadden many of us who were called to the bar in a kinder, gentler era, there is also reason for optimism. This author thinks it likely that a profitable new specialty area in litigation will develop—representing Ingrates from other law firms in their intra-firm disputes.

---

[*]Mr. Nuttree is one of the most important partners of the law firm of Fairweather, Winters & Sommers, 777 East Boulevard West, Chicago, Illinois 60611. Mr. Nuttree's direct dial number is 312-777-7776 and his car phone number is 708-864-7776. Potential paying clients should feel free to call any time.

Mr. Nuttree was ably assisted in preparation of this article by associates Verna Blender, Robert Hayes, and Jack Strauss of the Fairweather firm. Mr. Nuttree was less ably assisted in preparation of this article by associates Olivia Prescott, Henry Thompson, and Bruce Dresnett, who will probably not be with the Fairweather firm very much longer.

[1]As statistics in many different articles and publications too numerous to cite here show conclusively, the number of lawsuits filed in the United States has more than quadrupled over a period of quite a number of years.

[2]Those wishing a list of some of my victorious cases may call my secretary, Ludmilla, at 312-777-7787.

[3]See the Constitution of the United States and various federal papers written by famous colonists like Madison and Hamilton.

[4]See the Magna Carta and the Code of Hamurabi. Actually, the Code of Hamurabi is not technically a document, but rather a large slab of stone, which makes it very difficult to check out of the library.

[5]For example, as one of my clients wrote to me recently, "Dear Nails: Nice to see you at the health club the other day. Put on a little weight, haven't you? I've noticed the high cost of litigation."

[6]See my article entitled "Heads I Win, Tails You Lose: Flipping the Coin to Resolve Legal Disputes," 94 Harv L Rev 683 (1992).

[7]*Fairweather Alternative Dispute System: The Complete Rules and Regulations*, published by Fairweather Press, Nails Nuttree, editor. Call Samantha Priddy in the Fairweather library if you need a copy. If she can find it, she'll reproduce it for our normal photocopy charge of $.85 per page.

[8]Some Ingrates have complained that this rule is unfair, but such complaint has been dismissed by the Executive Committee as "just another example of the type of whining that goes on around this place." See Executive Committee minutes, June 20, 1993, in a folder marked "Miscellaneous Unimportant Documents" in Stanley Fairweather's lower left desk drawer. If they're not there, ask Bertha where he put them.

[9]Ibid.

[10]Metaphorically speaking, as there is no jury under FADS.

Reception Lines

by Gladys Jensen

SO ANYWAY, I'm sitting there one day, 54th-floor reception, and this guy comes in, a client I suppose. He walks up to me and says, "Mr. Helman to see Mrs. Barker."

And I say, "Is Mrs. Barker expecting you?"

And he says, "Not exactly, but I'm sure she'll see me. Just tell her Fred Helman is here."

So I say, "I'm afraid Mrs. Barker is not seeing anyone today."

But he doesn't give up, "Is she in?" he asks.

And I say, "No, Mrs. Barker is not in now."

So he goes right on, "Will she be back soon?"

So finally I have to tell him, "Not likely. Mrs. Barker passed away four weeks ago."

Well, of course Mr. Helman is a bit surprised at that news, but undaunted. "She should have seen me last time I was here," he says.

When I ask what he means by that, he explains that he is a life insurance salesman who has been encouraging Mrs. Barker to increase her coverage for years. And he asks me whether there are any other partners in the firm in the office that day "around the age of the late Mrs. Barker."

So that's life in the reception bizz. Not that we have people asking for deceased partners every day. It's probably only about twice a week. Just kidding. But you'd be surprised how many people we get who are trying to sell something or another to people at the firm. And they're pretty darn clever about it, too.

We had this fellow who used to pose as a messenger from Speedy-Serve Messenger Service. He would come to the reception desk and say that he was there to deliver an envelope to this or that attorney at our firm. Then once he got past the receptionist, he would go door-to-door trying to peddle everything from hot wristwatches to adult movies. We'd have caught this guy several months earlier than we did except for the fact that quite a number of our lawyers found his prices quite attractive and his merchandise of high quality.

This is no laughing matter, since we at the reception desks are the first line of defense for the security of the firm. To protect that security, we are authorized by the Fairweather Receptionist Manual to "exercise all necessary and reasonable force."

Our first defense is to ask somebody who is about to enter our space, "Excuse me, but may I help you?" This deters most criminals. If that fails, our next line of defense is to repeat the same words, only MUCH LOUDER. If neither of these works, the Receptionist Manual advises us to try one of the following:

1. apply the karate techniques you learned during receptionist training to flip the offender over the reception desk and into the wall directly behind it;

2. call the building security office by looking up the number, which is someplace in that little book that must be around here somewhere;

3. take out your bamboo shooter and blow a poison dart into the offender;

4. inquire as to how greatly the offender values his kneecaps;

5. press the button behind your desk, which will sound an alarm that will cause at least forty lawyers to be

trampled to death in the crowd that rushes into the reception area to ask, "What the hell was that?"

We tried to beef up our security after the firm hired Chief Fitzpatrick. The firm had a pedal installed on the floor underneath all the receptionists' desks, which we could step on when a suspicious-looking person entered the reception area. Pushing down the pedal caused a red light to flash in the Chief's office, signaling him to come running to our aid. We unhooked the pedal system, though, when clients objected to seeing a 6'4" Irishman burst into the reception area with his pistol drawn and shouting, "Keep calm and no one's gonna get hurt."

Getting back to poor Mrs. Barker, though, at least she died with her boots on. Or, more accurately, with one boot on. It was February and snowing to beat the band. Mrs. Barker was seated at her desk, leaning over to pull off her boots, and had gotten halfway when her Maker called her. She wasn't discovered until later in the day, when somebody brought in an interviewee from Harvard Law School. In case you're wondering, the interviewee did accept our firm's offer. She said that Mrs. Barker had not been noticeably less responsive to her questions than the other interviewers she'd seen at our firm that day.

Of course, one of our biggest challenges as receptionists is keeping track of our lawyers. First step is just knowing everyone in the office. For the attorneys, at least we have a picture book (or "pig book," as we affectionately refer to it). To help us perform our tasks, we have developed an extensive, high-tech continuing receptionist training program. Each receptionist is required to pass a test every six months in which slides of attorneys—front, back, and side views—are flashed up on a screen at half-second intervals, and the receptionist must identify every attorney until she reaches a 97% accuracy-rate. Another test requires receptionists to carry on a conversation with somebody standing in front of them, while at the same time watching a video screen of lawyers at the firm going in various directions. Receptionists must then answer questions regarding which attorneys appeared in the video, what directions they were going in, and whether they were returning to their office.

It's not just lawyers we need to keep track of, though, it's everyone. In fact, it's not the lawyers who are the toughest to deal with, it's the secretaries—especially secretaries of partners—who think they rule the heavens and the earth (not all of them, of course). We receptionists are supposed to know exactly where everyone on our floor is at every minute. The other day I had a secretary of a partner up here looking for an associate. She asked me where the associate was, and I told her that I thought I had seen him waddle into the men's room. She actually asked me how long I thought he'd be.

Not that we receptionists don't recognize the importance of knowing where our attorneys are. In fact, we at the Fairweather firm have developed a system to help us keep track of all our attorneys. The west wall of each reception area is covered with a large metal map of the office, the city, and the world. Each attorney has a magnetic likeness which we move around to indicate our latest information regarding that attorney's whereabouts.

Of course, with the advances in technology, we may not be so far from the time when we can do away with having to move magnets around and still know exactly where each attorney is at every minute. All attorneys will walk around with a tiny monitor in their briefcases that will allow us at the reception desk to track on a screen exactly where they are at all times.

Of course, it's very important for us receptionists to appear friendly. We're taught to smile and greet everyone with "Good morning [or afternoon], may I help you?" Some of our former receptionists found that script unduly stifling, and experimented with their own greetings, which ranged from, "Hey Toots, what's happenin'?" to "How very good of you to visit us this day. If there is any small way in which I may be of assistance, do not hesitate to give me a holler." Neither of those variations found particular favor with the partners, and their originators have been dispatched to positions for which Lt. Colonel Clinton L. Hargraves, CPA believes they may be better suited.

Though being a receptionist has its problems, it does help you to hone your powers of observation. As Yogi Berra used to say, "you can observe a lot by just looking." And we receptionists have a lot of time to look. In fact, an experienced receptionist ought to be able to identify who has come into the reception area without even asking. For example:

An attorney at the firm—just nods or makes a quick wave with the hand

An opposing attorney—carries large black box-like document case, does not smile, asks to use phone

A client—picks up copy of *Wall Street Journal, Forbes,* or *Barrons*; looks around and assesses the contents of the reception area as if he had paid for a major portion of it

A messenger—wears uniform, bounces his head up and down, cannot hear what you say to him because of earphones in ears

An attorney's spouse—does not tell you name since expects to be recognized, even if you have never seen them before

An interviewee—nervous, asks for washroom before giving you name; the only person who picks up and appears to read any firm brochures that are out on the coffee table

A salesperson—calls you by the name on the name-

plate on your desk; compliments you on the floral arrangement

Exactly what we should use these powers of observation for is not so clear, but I don't think they hurt. If
nothing else, they help us pass the time of day.

What's Up, Docket?

by Katherine Zyclops

WE IN DOCKET were born of adversity. In fact, the worst sort of adversity—the M-word: malpractice. Let me tell you how it happened.

It used to be that each attorney at our firm kept track of his own schedule. Everyone developed his own system for doing that. Some wrote key dates in their personal calendars, some wrote them on little slips of paper, some told their secretaries to remind them, some tied strings around their fingers, and some just remembered. Truth was, nobody had too many dates to remember back then anyway; we weren't all that busy. And even if you forgot about something, it wasn't that important because opposing counsel wouldn't make a big deal about it. After all, they might be the one who forgot next time.

But all that changed the day Hiram Miltoast sent his mother-in-law flowers.

Quality Credit Corporation was Hiram's biggest client, had been for many years. QCC was embroiled in a nasty class action brought by a group of borrowers who thought that QCC was charging them a lot more interest than was due. Those borrowers were not the type who would be inclined to excuse an innocent mistake on the part of opposing counsel.

Mr. Miltoast found that out when his mother-in-law, Suzie Franklin, called, somewhat puzzled, to thank him for the lovely flowers he had sent her. "Whatever are they for?" she asked.

"They're for your birthday, of course," said Hiram.

"But that's not for three weeks," she told him.

Hiram was stunned for a moment, then shouted into the phone, "Oh, no. That means that today must have been the date our reply brief was due in the case of *Franklin v. Quality Credit Corporation.*"

Indeed, it *was* the date the brief was due. And when the plaintiffs refused to extend the date, judgment was entered against QCC. And QCC, not being too pleased about that, hired new counsel and brought a malpractice suit against the Fairweather firm, which QCC won.

After the QCC fiasco, the firm set up a diary into which notations of all court cases, deadlines, etc. were to be entered. At first, Fairweather lawyers were dragged kicking and screaming into using this new procedure (the way, come to think of it, they've been dragged into every new procedure). In time, however, they began to see the myriad of possibilities for this system and began to use it in ways it was never intended to be used. When my docket staff began complaining to me about some of these instances, and some of the incredibly inefficient things our attorneys did, at first the Executive Committee did not believe what I reported to them. To prove that our complaints were justified, we in the docket department began recording some of the phone calls we received. Transcripts of some of these phone conversations are reproduced below:

Attorney: Which route do you take on your way to the federal courthouse?

Docket: We go straight down Adams.

Attorney: Then you go right by 125 West Adams?

Docket: Yes we do.

Attorney: Could you send somebody down to my office then, because I have a few shirts that I'd like you to drop off at the cleaners. I'd like them on hangers, with extra starch. And I need them by the day after to-morrow.

Docket: But . . .

Attorney: Thanks a lot.

* * *

Docket: We've made those copies of the entire court file on your case. It was a couple hundred pages, would you like us to bring them down to you now?

Attorney: Oh, didn't I tell you? I got a copy of that file from the opposing attorney. You can just throw yours away. And, by the way, don't bill the client—it was our mistake.

Docket: Our mistake?

Attorney: [click]

* * *

Attorney: Can you make sure that you get this answer on file today.

Docket: Why do you need it filed today?

Attorney: Well, today's March 5th. The complaint was filed on February 3rd, February has twenty-eight days so that means today is thirty days since the complaint was filed.

Docket: That's really excellent addition, but under the court rules, you have ninety days to answer the complaint.

Attorney: Oh, they just changed that?

Docket: Yes, just — in 1972.

* * *

Secretary: Mr. Flack's office.

Docket (breathing heavily): Yes, we just got back from the courthouse on the special rush trip that Mr. Flack asked us to make to get a copy of the complaint in the General Fixtures case. Do you want to come down and get it, or should we bring it up to your office?

Secretary: Oh, you can put it in the interoffice mail; Mr. Flack just left for vacation and won't be back for three weeks.

* * *

Attorney: Can you please advise me why in the world you scheduled my hearing on the motion to dismiss for Monday, June 23 at 2 P.M.

Docket: While there are several reasons we chose to schedule the hearing at that time, the principal one was your memo to us of May 14, which read, "Please schedule a hearing on my motion to dismiss for Monday, June 23 at 2 P.M."

* * *

Attorney: I got to that deposition and the deponent was not there. When I called him, he said that you had not served him with the subpoena.

Docket: We don't serve subpoenas.

Attorney: You don't?

Docket: No, and we don't do windows either.

* * *

Secretary: Mr. Phelps' office, good morning.

Docket: Can you tell me how we can reach Mr. Phelps?

Secretary: No, I'm afraid Mr. Phelps is on vacation.

Docket: We know that, but he left us a message that his secretary would know where to reach him.

Secretary: Oh, I'm sorry, I'm not his regular secretary. She's on vacation this week, too.

Docket: Did she leave a message where she could be reached?

Secretary: No, she said Mr. Phelps knew where to reach her if he needed to.

* * *

Attorney: Hello, is this docket?

Docket: Yes.

Attorney: Oh good.

Docket: May we help you?

Attorney: Not now, I just wanted to know I could reach you.

Docket: We're here when you need us.

Attorney: That's so comforting.

* * *

Attorney: What day of the week does Labor Day fall on this year?

Docket: This year, they're going to try holding Labor Day on a Monday, just to see how it works out.

* * *

Attorney: I've misplaced the copy of the stamped affidavit that you made from the file of *Jones v. Extra Big Corporation.* Could you please have somebody run over to court and make a copy for me from the file?

Docket: We'll send one right up. We always make an extra copy of whatever we give to you, since the odds are overwhelming that you will misplace it.

* * *

Attorney: Could you have someone come down here to pick up this motion, and get it filed today?

Docket: But it's ten minutes to five, and the clerk's office closes at five.

Attorney: Well, that gives you ten minutes.

Docket: But it takes twenty minutes to get over to the courthouse.

Attorney: But I told the client I would get it filed today.

Docket: Well, I guess you lied.

Well, those are only a few examples of what we in the docket put up with on a day-to-day basis. I'd tell you more about them, except that I've got a couple important calls to make. I've got to call Mr. Miltoast to remind him to send some flowers. It's Suzie Franklin's birthday tomorrow.

Hitting Nails on the Head

by Fricka Escher

As FAIRWEATHER, Winters & Sommers' marketing director, I try my darndest to generate publicity for the firm. One way I do that is by issuing daily press releases, utilizing the form firm press release that was drafted by COME, our Committee on Marketing Efforts.

FOR IMMEDIATE RELEASE:

ANOTHER VICTORY FOR FAIRWEATHER'S

In yet another stunning victory for the prestigious, highly-successful, client-oriented Fairweather, Winters & Sommers law firm, partner _____ [won a huge jury verdict, successfully defended a multi-million dollar lawsuit, closed an enormous business deal, buried another wealthy estate planning client] today. Reached for comment, _____ said, "Sure it was a stupendous accomplishment. But that sort of thing's all in a day's work here at the Fairweather firm." For further information, contact Fairweather marketing director, Fricka Escher.

On a particularly slow day, one of those releases may get picked up as filler in the local law bulletin.

Occasionally, though, I strike real pay dirt by getting

a prominent national legal periodical to do a feature story on one of our Fairweather lawyers. Unfortunately, however, there's a risk associated with that—I'm not always able to control the content of the articles I generate. For example, reprinted below is an article published in a recent issue of *The UnAmerican Lawyer* that caused quite a stir around the firm.

Nails Hammers Home Client Development

When Seymour "Nails" Nuttree joined Chicago's prestigious Fairweather, Winters & Sommers in 1968, it was just a large firm going no place fast. Thanks to Nails, though, it's now on the map.

Unlike some heavy hitters, Nails Nuttree does not believe in working behind the scenes. "Sure, I need stagehands, too. Even Nails can't do it all himself," Nails admits, modestly. "That's why I've got partners." Nails' attitude has not made him especially popular among his partners, as some are quick to admit in private. But all of Nails' partners respect his accomplishments.

"When one man is responsible for billing over $20 million annually, you tend to listen to what he says," admits corporate partner T. William Williams. A little over a year ago, T-Bills was forced to give up his office when Nails (his next door neighbor) decided he could use some more room and ordered the firm's administrator, Lt. Colonel Clinton Hargraves, CPA, to create an antechamber out of T-Bills' office. Unfortunately, when the first jackhammer crashed through the wall, T-Bills was discussing the defense of a tender offer with a new client. Mr. Williams makes light of the incident. "I'd have wanted the client to meet Nails, anyway. This just saved us the bother of having to go next door to do it." In private, though, T-Bills has confided to friends at FW&S that he was "just a little hurt and embarrassed at the way Nails handled the situation."

To find out how Nails pulls in his tremendous volume of business, *UnAmerican Lawyer* convinced Nails to let us spend a day with him. Here's our account.

As the sun rose over Nails Nuttree's 14-acre estate in Chicago's fashionable Lake Forest suburb, Nails was fast asleep. We talked to Nails' wife Carmela and his son Seymour Jr. ("Little Nails") and daughter Seymourina (also "Little Nails") about their perceptions of their husband and father.

"I'd describe Nails as strong-willed," Carmela says. "For instance, when he decided it was time for him and me to tie the knot, he sent Hurry Lopes and some of his boys from the firm's messenger corps over to the house at around nine one evening, told me and my folks to hop into the car for a little ride, and had us delivered to the church. I'd hoped to have a chance to pretty up a little beforehand, but I was so thrilled to be Mrs. Nails Nuttree, I didn't mind."

Little Nails and Little Nails both say they are extremely proud of their daddy. "When I grow up I'm hoping to be a lawyer, just like Big Nails," says Seymourina, "but if Daddy decides something else would be better for me, that's fine, too."

After the Little Nailses left for school, Carmela walked with us around the Nuttree estate. When we walked past the tennis court, she pointed out that one side of the court was a foot-and-a-half shorter and narrower than the other. "That's Nails' side," she explained. "He's a big man and it's difficult for him to cover a full-sized court. And Nails likes to win both in Federal court and on the tennis court. Most of the folks he plays with don't object."

Down the hill we came to a large muddy area with a

wire fence around it. As we approached, we noticed a hippopotamus in the center of the mud. "That's Slianie," explains Mrs. Nuttree. "Nails backwards with an 'ie' tacked on. One of the neighbors used to kid Nails about looking a little like a hippo. Nails has a marvelous sense of humor, so he decided to buy one and put it right near the neighbor's house to show 'em what a hippo really looks like. 'Course we needed a zoning variance, but that wasn't a big problem. Nails represents the zoning board."

By 11:00 A.M., Nails was downstairs and, after a quick orange juice, Denver omelette, order of English, rasher of bacon, side of country-fried potatoes, and two waffle "chasers," as Nails put it, we were on our way to his limousine, a black Cadillac with "Nails" written in orange script on each door. The bartender offered us each a drink as the stretch limo pulled from the curb. Nails accepted a double martini with seven olives and cocktail onions. We opted for Shirley Temples, explaining that we had to write up our article that afternoon.

Between car-phone calls from opposing counsel wanting to settle a large environmental case he was handling, Nails spoke proudly of the changes he had brought to the Fairweather firm. When Nuttree arrived, it was well known in Chicago legal circles that his firm had a terrible problem collecting its accounts receivable. "Other firms were futzin' around with imposing interest charges and the like," Nails explains. "Others were suing their clients. Now I'm a litigator, but collecting your fees that way takes a lot of time and effort. So I decided to focus on kneecaps instead of law suits. Most clients really like their kneecaps and if they feel that they are in the slightest bit of danger of being bashed in, they tend to pay their bills, pronto."

We stepped from Nails' limo into the firm's office building and rode the elevator to 72, known, we later learned, as Nails Country. Nails' office occupied approxi-

mately one-quarter of the floor; the balance was devoted to litigation associates and paralegals who provided Nails-support. After checking with his secretary, Ludmilla, on the morning's receipts, Nails led us on a tour of the office. We murmured our approval at two floors tastefully done in bastard-modern law office, but we gasped at the contrast offered by the third floor we visited.

"When I came here, we had a reputation as a sweat-shop," Nuttree chuckles. "When I investigated the cause of that reputation, I found out our own associates were say-ing it. So I figured, hell, if they want sweatshop, I'll give 'em sweatshop. I had two of our floors cleared out, no interior walls, no offices, no nothing, just some metal desks and plastic palms, set up in rows. We moved our associates down there and gave them specific goals to work toward. We told them how many contracts, wills, answers to interrogatories and the like we'd appreciate their turn-ing out each day. Sure, it meant that we couldn't attract those precious students at the top of their classes in the fancy Ivy League law schools, but hell, our work doesn't really demand that anyway. Some of my partners are chimpanzees. So we went to the middle and bottom of classes around the country and fished us out some real workers. And they don't complain much about the working conditions and hours, either."

After our tour, Nails invited us to join him for lunch at the Bigwig Club on the 66th floor of the building. When the maître d' informed Nails that no window tables were available, Nails walked over to a table near the window and spoke to its occupants. He returned to tell us that two of his partners and their clients had graciously offered to change tables so that we might enjoy a view of downtown Chicago and Lake Michigan.

Over lunch, Nails downed two more mega-martinis. From time to time he excused himself to greet the occupants of other tables. Between these trips, Nails explained to us that, though he was a powerful figure in the firm, he had always been prepared to share power with his partners. In fact, he has shunned a spot on the Fairweather Executive Committee: "I prefer to let others have their say. I'm told that I can sometimes be a little intimidating, so I stay away from Executive Committee meetings. After each meeting, I just have one or two members come into my office to tell me what was decided. Then I tell them whether we're going to do it or not. It works well. Saves me sitting through all of them dumb meetings."

Nails also steers clear of the typical internal squabbles over partnership shares. "I don't have time for that, and the diddly squat differences in percentage that my partners worry about don't interest me. I just tell them what I need and they're free to divvy up the rest any way they want."

After lunch, Nails invited us to join him for a spot of client hunting. We limoed over to the offices of Sidley & Austin, one of Fairweather's principal competitors. In the elevator up, Nuttree took a red mustache from his coat pocket, pasted it under his nose, and slipped on a pair of wire-rimmed glasses that he pulled from his inside coat pocket. As we debarked the elevator, the receptionist asked if she could help us. Nails told her no, he was "just looking."

As clients of Sidley came into the reception area and sat down, Nails struck up conversations with them. We were not close enough to hear the conversations, but we watched each client get up, leave, and wait near the elevators.

After Nails had rounded up six clients, he took us and them in his limousine back to the Fairweather firm. Nails announced to the receptionist that this was "today's batch." He asked her to please usher them into the client detention conference room and to get somebody in there, find out what their problems were, and get a lawyer to service them.

Back in his own office, Nails confided to us that Sidley and other firms were starting to get wise to him and had circulated his picture to their receptionists. But thus far that had proved unsuccessful. "I've got me a set of wigs and false mustaches, different colors and everything," Nails confides. "I never wear the same one two days in a row." Nuttree admits that one of these days the other firms will penetrate his disguise, but he is not afraid. "We're gonna just blast our way into the lawyers' offices and kidnap the clients. I've already got an opinion from the Illinois State Bar that it's ethical or, if not ethical, at least protected by the First Amendment."

Stanley Fairweather was not amused by the *UnAmerican Lawyer* article, and summoned me and Nails into his office. He told me that he thought all future contact with the press ought to be through a designated firm spokesman; and he designated himself. He asked Nails about the numerous inaccuracies in the article attributable to direct quotes from him, and quizzed him about the reports Stanley had gotten from Hurry Lopes in the mailroom that Nails had been circulating reprints of the article to friends and clients. Nails allowed as how he might have gotten a little carried away in describing his role in the firm to the *UnAmerican Lawyer* reporters, and promised to destroy all remaining reprints. Stanley said he thought that Nails might relate better to the stagehands and chimpanzees in the firm if Nails' compensation were cut by a diddly squat twenty-five percent. Nails said he thought that was a good idea. And, finally, Stanley offered Nails two words that he thought would help Nails handle all of his future calls from the press—"no comment."

You Can Count on That

SOME TIME AGO, when the Fairweather firm was searching for a comptroller, it interviewed Orville Figuremeister, a leading candidate for the position by reason of his background as a CPA and his extremely boring resume. Because of security measures instituted by Chief Brian Fitzpatrick, all interviews with prospective employees at the firm are tape recorded. Set forth below is a transcript of the interview that Lieutenant Colonel Clinton L. Hargraves, CPA conducted with Mr. Figuremeister.

HARGRAVES: C'mon in, have a seat. I'm Lieutenant Colonel Clinton L. Hargraves, CPA, but why don't you just call me Clint.

FIGUREMEISTER: I'm Orville Figuremeister, but I go by Orv. Actually, my friends call me Figs.

HARGRAVES: Well, my friends call me Stinky, but we're not friends yet, are we Orville?

FIGUREMEISTER: No, I guess we're not, but I hope that maybe someday we will be.

HARGRAVES: Well, we'll have to see about that. How about a little nip? I keep a bottle in my desk drawer.

FIGUREMEISTER: No thanks, I never drink before eleven.

HARGRAVES: Well, okay, suit yourself. So you want to be a comptroller?

FIGUREMEISTER: Yes, I do. I've always wanted to be a comptroller, ever since I was a little kid. I've read biographies of all of the famous comptrollers in history. And Mom and Dad took me to visit the comptroller's hall of fame in Sandusky, Ohio when I was only seven.

HARGRAVES: Good with numbers, are you, Figuremeister?

FIGUREMEISTER: Eight times four equals thirty-two. Eighty-three minus twenty-seven equals fifty-six.

HARGRAVES: Pretty good.

FIGUREMEISTER: Wait, you haven't seen anything yet. Twenty-seven divided by nine, times eighteen, equals fifty-four. Square root of sixteen, times seven, divided by two, minus nine, equals five.

HARGRAVES: Very impressive.

FIGUREMEISTER: Go ahead, ask me anything.

HARGRAVES: Well, let me see . . . If Mary was one-half the age of John on her last birthday and John was six years older than Susan, how old is Mary if the sum of John and Susan's ages is twelve more than Mary's age?

FIGUREMEISTER: Easy, six. Here's one for you. Ben and Lucy are both starting from city A in separate cars, heading to city B, which is one hundred miles from city A. Ben starts out two hours before Lucy and drives at thirty miles per hour. Assuming that Ben stops along the way for forty-five minutes and Lucy drives at fifty miles per hour without stopping, which of them will arrive at city B first and how far will the other one be from city B at the time the first arrives?

HARGRAVES: Lucy will arrive first, of course, and Ben will be two-and-a-half miles away.

FIGUREMEISTER: Hey, not bad for an old man.

HARGRAVES: Thanks, but, you know, this is not really the type of math that we need here at the firm.

FIGUREMEISTER: It isn't? Well, what kind of math do you need? I can do solid geometry—the volume of a cylinder equals pi times the radius squared, times length. And I was a wiz at trig—the tangent . . .

HARGRAVES: No, I'm afraid that won't help, either. What we need to know is how to boost our profits.

FIGUREMEISTER: Well, why didn't you say so? Nothing easier, just increase your revenues.

HARGRAVES: That's easier said than done. How?

FIGUREMEISTER: Increase the number of clients.

HARGRAVES: But every firm is trying to do that. How can we succeed?

FIGUREMEISTER: Do more marketing.

HARGRAVES: But marketing costs money, so that will reduce our profits.

FIGUREMEISTER: Maybe in the short term, but it will increase them in the long run.

HARGRAVES: Long run, hah, what's that? We're talking about a law firm, here, Figuremeister. We pay out all our profits every year. There *is* no long run.

FIGUREMEISTER: Okay then, just increase the number of hours each attorney bills.

HARGRAVES: But our attorneys are already complaining that they're working too many hours.

FIGUREMEISTER: Then raise your hourly rates.

HARGRAVES: We can't get away with that anymore. Our clients are very cost conscious, and not very loyal. They'll leave us and go to other firms.

FIGUREMEISTER: Okay, if you can't increase revenues, then slash expenses.

HARGRAVES: Good idea, but how are we going to do that?

FIGUREMEISTER: Just take a look at your big ticket items— what are they?

HARGRAVES: Associate salaries.

FIGUREMEISTER: Great, that makes it easy. All you have to do is fire a bunch of your associates.

HARGRAVES: But doing that would reduce the number of billable hours for the firm and cut our profit.

FIGUREMEISTER: Okay then, keep all of your associates, but cut all of their salaries by twenty-five percent.

HARGRAVES: If we do that, they'll leave the firm and that will have the same effect on reducing billable hours as firing them.

FIGUREMEISTER: Okay then, let's leave associates alone, forget about them. What's your next biggest expense?

HARGRAVES: Rent.

FIGUREMEISTER: No problem, then, move to less expensive space.

HARGRAVES: But our attorneys have gotten used to these quarters. Besides, they think it helps us attract wealthy clients. And the move itself would cost so much that we couldn't do that, even if we wanted to.

FIGUREMEISTER: Then renegotiate the lease.

HARGRAVES: We did that two years ago, and now we've got twenty-three years left on our new lease, so the landlord is not likely to renegotiate again at this point.

FIGUREMEISTER: Well, if we can't cut the big items, then maybe we've got to whittle away very slowly at some of the smaller expense items, but that will take quite a bit of time.

HARGRAVES: You're hired.

FIGUREMEISTER: I'm what? I don't understand. Why am I hired? I haven't solved any of your firm's problems.

HARGRAVES: Do you think I want to hire somebody as comptroller who can come in here with quick solutions to all the problems we've been wrestling with for a decade? How would that make me or our Finance Committee or Executive Committee look?

FIGUREMEISTER: Pretty stupid, I guess.

HARGRAVES: Darn right, and we have plenty of things that make us look that way without the help of a new comptroller.

FIGUREMEISTER: So you want me to just sort of plod along

with the same old solutions that haven't worked all these years?

HARGRAVES: I think you're getting the idea, now. Any objection to that approach . . . Figs?

FIGUREMEISTER: None at all, Stinky.

HARGRAVES: Good, then how about that drink?

FIGUREMEISTER: Make mine a double.

[EDITOR'S NOTE: Figuremeister has worked out just as Hargraves anticipated. Though he has not solved any of the firm's financial problems, Figs and his staff of five stand ready to tackle any problem, no matter how small or insignificant.]

The Proof's in the Pudding

by Dr. Isidore Q. Hobsworthy

SURE, at one time I might have expected that my Ph.D. in English from Harvard would land me in an idyllic spot in some ivy-covered, red-brick classroom building of a prestigious East Coast institution of higher learning, ensconced behind a metal desk stacked high with books and papers, scooting around on my old wooden desk chair, the kind with the coasters that leave those indelible black streaks in the flecked linoleum floor of my musty, book-lined, cinder-block walled office, the bottom half of the window that looks out from my office onto the criss-crossed walks of the quadrangle below open inward forty-five degrees and the blond wood door, Scotch-taped with my schedule of office hours and pithy New Yorker cartoons, just slightly ajar. But things don't always work out the way you expect.

So when the job market for English majors, especially Chaucer specialists, dried up a bit—quite a bit, in fact—I answered an ad for head of the proofreading department at Fairweather, Winters & Sommers. I was married and had a small child at the time, so I needed work. I darn near didn't get the job, though, because the head of the word-processing department, Mary Shipmore, under whose jurisdiction proofreading fell, thought I was over qualified. Fortunately, though, Mary was impressed enough with me to call Mr. Fairweather, who asked her to bring me down to his office. And after an hour or so of talking about the Miller's Tale, the Reeve's Tale, and the Wife of Bath, Mr. Fairweather brought me back up to Mary's office and told her he'd hired me. As I recall, he said, "we could use a few over-qualifieds around here. It would balance us out."

And I'm happy. My perspective has changed quite a bit. I used to read Chaucer for pleasure. The other day I came across a volume and all I could see were the typos. Just about every other word had an extra "e" tacked on to it. Yes, Chaucer seems a long way off now.

We've had quite a few changes in the Fairweather proofreading department since I took over eight years ago. In fact, we're no longer the proofreading department at all, we're the editorial department. And that's more than a mere change in name. Like most of the things around the Fairweather firm, the change came about because of Stanley. Here's how it happened.

When I arrived, my department corrected the spelling and punctuation of documents, but left everything else as is—no matter how horrible it was. Of course, those of us in the department would snicker over some of the stuff that came through. In fact, we established awards— Dullitzer Prizes we called them—for documents in various categories. Those prizes were awarded semi-annually in secret ceremonies in our department. One day, though, our cover was blown when Stanley Fairweather happened upon us laughing hysterically during one of our award ceremonies. As I recall, we were awarding a Dullitzer to the trust and estates department for the following provision:

> Notwithstanding the other provisions of the will of which this Article that you are now reading is a part and which is incorporated fully herein, and no matter what those other provisions say or how clear those other provisions may seem, if any legatee is under the age of twenty-one at my death, which death I hope is a long way off, the interest of such beneficiary ("the Kid") shall be vested, suited and dressed up, but distribution of the property and appurtenances thereto bequeathed here-

with shall not be made to the Kid because the Kid more likely than not will just piss the property and appurtenances bequeathed herewith away. Now, therefore, instead, distribution shall be made as follows, to wit: to any parent, grandparent, uncle, aunt, long-lost cousin or other relative having custody of the Kid designated as Trustee by the Executor. The Trustee shall hold, manage, protect, preserve and distribute such interest as a separate, independent and isolated trust which shall terminate when the Kid becomes such age or, heaven forbid, dies, perishes, passes on or otherwise meets his or her Maker before becoming such age. Until the termination, completion, collapse, disintegration or other end of such trust, the Trustee may retain or sell and invest the proceeds of all or any part of such property and appurtenances and shall distribute to or for the support, benefit and distinct advantage of the Kid such portions of the income, principal and corpus of such trust as the Trustee may from time to time determine to be reasonably needed, desirable or come in handy for such purpose. On the termination or other end or conclusion of such trust, the Trustee shall distribute the principal of such trust to the Kid if living and if not living, to the estate of the Kid, so long as everybody getting a distribution is a life in being and doesn't violate the Rule Against Perpetuities. In lieu of making distribution to such Trustee, the Executor may designate any individual, bank, corporation, partnership, trust or gerbil, wherever situated, as custodian for the Kid under a Uniform Transfers (or Gifts) to Minors (or Miners) Act or similar statute, law, regulation or constitution then in effect, and the custodian shall hold, manage and distribute such property in accordance with the provisions of such statute, law, regulation or constitution.

When Stanley asked us what was so funny, we showed him the trust provision and told him it was boilerplate in the standard office will. Stanley read it over twice and said he thought the whole thing pretty much came down to, "if the Kid isn't of age yet, let his parents or some other relative hold it for him until he turns twenty-one." I told him that was what we figured it meant, too.

Stanley asked whether we came across similar gibberish from other areas of the practice. When we assured him that we did, he asked us to collect examples and to meet with him again in two weeks. After he saw what we'd collected, he circulated the following memo:

To: All Lawyers
From: Stanley J. Fairweather
Subject: English

For most of us, English is our native language. We are taught to write it in our grammar schools, high schools, and universities. Then in law school, and in our practice, we are taught a new dialect that creeps into everything we write, making it completely indecipherable to non-lawyers. This phenomenon has been brought home to me recently by I. Q. Hobsworthy, head of our proofreading department, who showed me some of the products we have been turning out lately.

As you know, since Dr. Hobsworthy arrived, we have upgraded our proofreading department substantially. Currently it is staffed entirely with Ph.D.s in English. The department has been meeting periodically for some time now, awarding what they call Dullitzer Prizes to particularly poor examples of our prose. Effective immediately, I wish to announce the following policies:

1. English is hereby declared the official language of the Fairweather firm.

2. All communications to clients and within the firm, and all documents drafted by firm lawyers, shall use the firm's official language.

3. The proofreading department is hereby abolished, and in its place the editorial department is established.

4. Dullitzer Prizes shall be presented publicly by the editorial department to undeserving authors.

5. Dullitzer Prizes shall carry with them the privilege of making a large cash contribution to a fund, the amount of which shall be determined based upon the income of the author and the aggrievousness of the writing. Our Charitable Contributions Committee shall accumulate and invest those contributions and donate them to the first law school to abolish its legal writing program and replace it with an English-Writing for Lawyers program.

Stanley's memo was just the beginning of the change in our department's status at the firm. Geodfrey Bleschieu, of our Associates Committee, thought that our editorial department might be the answer to the perennial complaints we received from associates about lack of feedback from attorneys on their work. So, in addition to making editorial changes in the work that was turned in to our word-processing department, we were charged by the Associates Committee with giving each document submitted by an associate a grade. Where an associate was doing poor work, failing to turn work in, or behaving badly, we arranged for conferences with the associate's parents to discuss the problems. The grades we gave on documents were utilized in arriving at quarterly grades for each associate in the firm, thus allowing them to simulate what all associates wish for, deep down—that they never had to leave school. And as word of our grading system spread to the law schools, it increased the firm's recruiting success markedly.

Finally, Fricka Escher, of our marketing department, got the idea that the new policies announced in Stanley's memo would go over well with clients. She developed a promotional piece with a cover that proclaimed, "At Fairweather, Winters & Sommers, English Is Our Official Language," and which highlighted the academic prowess of our editorial department. Eventually, some of our clients were so impressed with the prose we turned out that they asked for help from our editorial department with their own communications. We now bill out that help at between $110 and $160 per hour, making our department more profitable than either our real estate or trusts and estates departments.

So you can see why I don't miss Chaucer much. Sure, maybe tenure would be nice. But that's unrealistic—nobody has tenure in a law firm anymore. And I have something better than all those professors with tenure, anyway—the confidence that I'm making a real contribution.

Going Out on a Branch

NOT LONG AGO, at the suggestion of firm marketing
director Fricka Escher, the firm engaged the prominent
consulting firm of Tellem, Wathey, Noh to take a look at
its branch office relations. Fricka's notion was that better
communication between the branches could enhance the
firm's marketing efforts. Here is a portion of the report
TWN submitted.

Introduction

You have asked us to review your relations with your
branch offices and to recommend methods of improving
communication. As you know, as law firms become larger
and more geographically dispersed, communication becomes both more difficult and more important. Effective
communication is a key to cross-selling clients in different
geographical areas. In other words, you are extremely
clever indeed to have engaged us at our hefty fee to review
this issue for you.

Analysis

We have analyzed your situation through a combination of (a) in-depth interviews with lawyers both in your
home office and in your branches, (b) questionnaires to
your lawyers, and (c) just plain, old-fashioned noodling.

Our extensive interviews confirmed that a communication problem of some magnitude in fact exists. To
illustrate, here are some representative comments made
by lawyers at your home office:

"You're kidding me, I didn't know we had an office there."

"How should I know what they do out there in the boonies? But I'll tell you this—whatever the hell it is, they're not making any money for us, that's for sure."

"I think we have one branch. No, wait a minute, maybe it's two; no, four . . . hang on a second, let me pull out my firm directory, if there is one."

Initially, we were unable to conduct interviews at your branch offices, since nobody at the home office seemed to know how to reach them. Acting on the suggestion of Lt. Colonel Clint Hargraves, CPA, however, we dialed information in several major cities around the country and asked whether they had a listing for a Fairweather, Winters & Sommers. In this way, we uncovered three branches, one of which had apparently been missing for more than six years.

Once we found them, lawyers in the branches told us in their interviews:

"They just don't understand us. All we want is a little love and attention. Is that too much to ask?"

"We're growing fast. Some day we'll be bigger than they are, and then we'll ignore *them* and see how *they* like it."

We believe that these and a few other things we heard that are a little too sick to repeat in this report reveal severe emotional problems in your branch-office partners. On a more positive note, however, this appears to put them squarely in the mainstream with their home-office brethren.

The apparent communication problem revealed by our interviews was confirmed by the results of the questionnaires that we sent out to all of your lawyers. For exam-

ple, in response to question #308, "Would you describe the level of communication between offices as (a) excellent, (b) good, (c) average, (d) fair, (e) poor?" none said that communication was excellent, 3% said that communication was good, 8% said average, 16% fair, 24% poor and 39% checked "none of the above" and penciled in comments such as "what communication?" "about the same as me and my ex-husband" and "semi-annual."

Recommendations

Having confirmed after three months of intensive work that a communication problem existed, we turned lickedy-split to the question of what the hell to do about it. In that vein, we considered several possible solutions, including the following:

- eliminate the communication problem by closing all branch offices immediately;
- require every lawyer in the home office to call at least three lawyers in each branch office every day, just to say "howdy-do;"
- circulate copies of all correspondence that goes out of any office to people in each of the other offices;
- conduct monthly retreats that bring together lawyers from all of the offices.

While each of these solutions had its particular charm or appeal, all were rejected as being either too radical, too expensive, or too dumb. Instead, we are recommending a two-pronged approach to improving communication between offices through, prong one, creating a firm newsletter and, prong two, placing a lawyer from outside the home office on the Executive Committee. I will discuss these prongs one at a time below (since I know how annoying two-at-a-time prong discussions can be).

Establishing a firm newsletter. This publication would provide a ready vehicle for communication between offices.

In order for this vehicle to work, though, there must be representation on the newsletter staff from each of the offices. (Unfortunately, however, since there is now virtually no communication between offices, we will need first to establish another vehicle for the staff members of the newsletter to communicate. To accomplish this, we recommend establishing a weekly newsletter-staff communication newsletter.)

Not surprisingly, the establishment of a newsletter raises many issues that will need to be resolved, among them:

- how frequently will the newsletter be published?
- what will the newsletter be called?
- who will edit the newsletter?
- will there be a funnies section?
- will the newsletter contain photographs?
- why will the newsletter contain photographs?
- who will write columns in the newsletter?
- what size will the newsletter be?
- how will the newsletter be distributed?
- how much will a subscription to the newsletter cost?

To resolve these and other questions, we recommend establishing a Firm Newsletter Committee, to be composed of all lawyers at the firm who wrote for their high school newspapers.

Branch office member on the Executive Committee. Everything important that happens at the Fairweather firm is resolved through the Executive Committee (unless, of course, in Stanley Fairweather's judgment, it's too important for the Executive Committee, in which case he decides it). Therefore, to assure communication, it is crucial that the branch offices have representation on the EC. The question is how to select the branch-office representative. We have noodled this one over quite a bit back here at the TWN office, and here's what we've come up with.

One approach would be to have the branch representative elected by all the partners. This would have the advantage of selecting someone who had the support of all the partners, but would not give the branch-office partners a direct say in choosing their representative.

Another approach would be to put the names of all branch-office partners into a hat and select one. This would have the advantage of being fair, but would not assure that a quality candidate would be selected.

A third approach would allow the branch-office partners to select their own representative by secret ballot. This, however, would almost certainly result in a tie, since each branch currently has only one partner.

A fourth approach would be to select the partner who has the largest billings. While this would assure selection of a heavy hitter, we all know that heavy hitters are generally the worst Executive Committee members.

A fifth approach (the "Senate Approach") would be to place a partner from each office on the Executive Committee. Though this would be fair and assure representation on the part of every office, it is about as likely to fly with the Executive Committee as would a plan to determine partnership compensation by weight.

We are left then with a choice of alternatives, all of which have something to commend themselves, but none of which is totally satisfactory. Our recommendation is to combine a number of the possibilities discussed above. To that end, we suggest that the names of branch-office partners be placed in a hat. Stanley Fairweather will then look at the names and select one out of the hat. This name will then be submitted on a ballot for a vote of both the entire partnership and the branch-office partners. We believe that this method will assure a quality Executive

Committee candidate, while preserving intact the firm's tradition of fairness and democracy.

[EDITOR'S NOTE: After reading the TWN report, Fricka Escher decided to focus her efforts on marketing in Fairweather's principal office, Chicago, and leave the branches for another day—she thought maybe March 24, 2057.]

Who's Spartacus?

by Mary Shipmore

QUICK, name three people in your word-processing department. How about two. Can't, can you. No, those of us in word processing toil in anonymity.

I'm not complaining, mind you. There are advantages to anonymity. When secretaries screw up, they hear about it directly. Lawyers may be plenty mad at us in word processing when we mess something up, but at least they have no idea which of us did it. (Or at least that was true until our anonymity was threatened, as you will see below.) And we refuse to tell.

For those of you old enough to remember the movie, we in word processing take the "I'm Spartacus" approach: we all accept blame for every mistake. (This is a stark contrast to our attorneys, who take the "You're Spartacus" approach, never accepting blame for anything.) Of course, in order to pull that off, you need a sense of cohesion in the department. As head of word processing, I try to build that team spirit through our weekly 7 A.M. Monday morning status meetings. Here is a transcript of last week's session.

"Is everyone here?"

"Of course not, it's only 7:15."

"But I thought we were supposed to start at 7."

"No, we just call the meeting for 7 so that we can start at 7:30."

"Then why don't we just call it for 7:30, and let everybody sleep half an hour longer."

"No, if we did that we wouldn't start until 8, and that would be too late."

"Well, I don't see why we can't just start our meetings on time."

"We do start them on time, it's just that the time we start them on does not happen to be the time we call them for."

"Never mind, please pass the donuts, Lucy."

"Mind if I take one first?"

"No, just save me a jelly-filled one."

"We don't have any of those."

"Why not? Those are my favorite."

"We're under orders from the Executive Committee: no more filled donuts. The litigation department was unhappy that there was jelly on several pages of their appellate brief to the Seventh Circuit in that big *Simmons* case."

"I'll bet that was because of the proofreaders; they never lick their fingers good like we do."

"That may be, but we're under strict orders not to buy jelly-filled donuts anymore."

"Why don't we get started with the meeting; the others will be along soon. How did the weekend go?"

[NOTE: Here several pages on the general topic of "who is doing what to whom" are deleted on the grounds they were irrelevant and, arguably, defamatory.]

"Well, we don't have much time left, why don't we review last week's problems."

"We got into a bind because we had rush jobs both on Nails Nuttree's big Seventh Circuit brief and on a law review article entitled, 'Jack's Spat Was Over Fat, His Wife's Was Over Liens.' "

"Yes, you should have seen Nails' little associates and their secretaries hovering around our department. They were like a flock of eagles soaring above us, looking for their prey."

"They learned it from Nails, you know; he used to be one of the truly great hoverers in his younger days. Now he just stays in his office, shouting a lot, and lets his underlings do the hovering."

"Maybe we should post NO HOVERING signs around the department."

"That would never work, but it might be fun to post somebody with a beebee gun in a corner of word processing to try to bring down a few of those eaglets."

"Actually, I don't understand what the problem was: Nails' brief should certainly have taken precedence over a law review article."

"But the law review article had to be in by the end of the week; there was a deadline."

"But still, Nails' work should have taken precedence."

"There is no question that Nails' work would take precedence; the question was *which* of Nails' work—the law review article was Nails' too."

"Well, why didn't you just ask Nails?"

"We did. But he told us he wasn't going to get in the middle of this one, we'd have to resolve it ourselves."

"So what did you do?"

"We wound up delaying the four thousand personal letters that we were sending out to clients, as part of the firm's marketing effort informing them all of an obscure change in a provision of the Internal Revenue Code relating to the deductibility of the cost of pesticides that were found to violate Environmental Protection Act standards. It seems that the shining light of our tax department, Emanuel Candoo, is co-chair of the Subcommittee on Pesticide Deductibility at the bar association. Manny's the recognized authority on this new provision, and our marketing director, Fricka Escher, wanted all of our clients to be aware of that."

"Well, that sounds like a good solution. Did Fricka have any problem with the delay?"

"Not really, but Mr. Candoo sure did. He was beside himself, spouting sections of the Internal Revenue Code and saying how it was crucial to get that letter out, because pesticide deductibility was 'on the tip of everyone's tongue' last week, and how important it is 'to strike while the iron is hot' on these types of things."

"So what did you do?"

"We asked Mr. Candoo whether he would like to talk to Nails about delaying his brief and his law review article."

"And what did he say?"

"He calmed down pretty quickly, said he'd let it go 'just this once,' if we were sure we could get it out this week."

"We're getting more and more backed up. We need to think about a new way of allocating the work."

"Maybe we should divide it up by departments, have different people in word processing specialize on jobs of different departments."

"That's not a bad idea, but the problem is we don't have enough different people to cover all the departments, and some departments have much greater needs for word processing help than others."

"Well, maybe we should divide the work up between 'rush' and 'non-rush' work."

[At this point, there were several minutes of unabated laughter.]

"What's so funny?"

"Non-rush? When did you ever see anything in word processing that was not a rush?"

"Okay, maybe we should leave the organization alone. Were there any other problems last week?"

"Yes, it was a big Nails week. Unfortunately, Edna made a serious mistake on another one of Nails' briefs, and he was furious."

"Well, that's too bad, but I assume that we adhered to department policy and didn't tell Nails who had made the mistake."

"Of course not, but he found out."

"How did he do that?"

"Well, Nails used to be with the U.S. Attorney's office, so he dusted the document for fingerprints, and that led him to Edna."

"That's terrible. We've got to figure out a way to avoid that in the future. We can't have our people responsible for their own mistakes. That would be terrible for morale."

"I've got an idea. Why don't we have everybody in the department handle each page of each document; that way they won't be able to trace who produced a particular document."

"Good idea, but there's one problem. If we passed every document around to everyone to be handled, it would slow things down so much that we'd have the entire firm on our back. We've got to come up with another way."

"What about this? We could get everyone in word processing to wear gloves. That way, Nails wouldn't be able to trace who had produced the document."

"Great idea, and it would eliminate another serious problem, too."

"What's that?"

"Well, if everybody wore gloves, maybe we could go back to ordering jelly-filled donuts."

"Why's that?"

"Simple. We eat the donuts with our fingers, then put the gloves on to keep the jelly off the documents."

"So the gloves get us out of two sticky situations at once."

"Yup, we can lick one, and also avoid getting fingered."

"Or pun-ished."

The Spice of Life

by Phillip D. W. Wilson III

OUR FIRM, like most other large law firms, has not
achieved the degree of diversity we might like in our
personnel. To try to improve our efforts, the Fairweather
Executive Committee appointed a Diversity Committee
and named me its chair. To kick off our renewed diversity
efforts, I called a meeting of all lawyers and staff at the
firm and delivered what one young associate who works in
my department and is dependent upon me for his work
and pay called "one heck of a fine keynote address." I have
given the editors my permission to reprint my keynote
speech here:

Brothers. Sisters. I welcome you. I would like to
acknowledge first off that I am a white male. There would
be no purpose served in trying to deny this. Just look at
me, I fairly reek of white maleness.

But I am no racist. To prove that, I would like to
announce that I have just resigned from the Bigwig Club
in protest against its policy of permitting no African-
American, American Indian, Asian, or Hispanic members
(with your permission, for convenience I'd like hereinafter
to refer to peoples in those ethnicities as "Those People").

You may ask why I did not resign from the Bigwig
earlier, since by looking around the club on any given day
one could see that none of Those People were present. The
plain fact is that I simply did not notice, since in my
neighborhood there are none of Those People either.
Brothers and sisters, I am ethnically disadvantaged.

Why, you might ask, would the firm choose me, a white male, as our director of diversity. Why not choose somebody of African-American, Asian, Hispanic, or American Indian descent. The reason, of course, is that we have none of Those People among our partners at present.

And why not, you may ask. I certainly don't want to appear defensive here. Throughout our history, our firm has always stood for nondiscrimination, equal opportunity for all, affirmative action, integration, diversity, and rooting for the underdog. That we currently have no minority partners is a matter of pure chance, and not the result of any invidious pattern of discrimination whatsoever. Anybody who says otherwise is a dirty rotten liar, a bigot, and a reverse discriminator of the worst type.

In fact, quite the opposite is true. Our Hiring Committee has gone out of its way to bag us two minority associates. For example, we recently hired Kareem Running Bear, who is half American Indian and half African-American. Kareem grew up in the Sudan, where his parents had emigrated to establish an all-night bowling alley. At age eleven, Kareem was spirited away to Israel by a Hassidic bowling team that was competing in his parents' establishment, and he was raised as an Orthodox Jew. Kareem is left-handed. And though we wouldn't mind having one or two more like Kareem, we've been frustrated in our efforts. With firms all over the country looking to stock up on minorities, and so few of Those People in our law schools, there simply are not enough to go around.

To prove that we hold no grudge against our brothers and sisters who were not fortunate enough to have been born white, you can see, looking around the room, that we have many minorities in our non-legal staff, though none of you have risen to the managerial level, as yet. To you I caution patience. These things take time. Rome was not built in a day.

But what is diversity anyway? Let's recognize here that diversity is a relative concept. If we were in, say, Japan right now, I, Phillip D. W. Wilson III, would add diversity to the picture.

How would you know that? Simple. I would just plain look different. I'd be taller, I wouldn't be wearing those fancy bathrobes and house slippers around, and I wouldn't always be snapping photographs.

Now let me stop myself right there. What I just said is bad, because it is based upon stereotypes. It's been years since all of the Japanese walked around in those outfits. And it may not have been the Japanese, anyway. It may have been the Chinese or Koreans. Who can tell them apart? And not all of them snap pictures; many of them, with their new affluence, are using videocams. But I still support free trade, and I, for one, am prepared to put World War II behind us. So these are the types of stereo-typical attitudes that we must fight to get away from, which is something we on the Fairweather diversity team are striving to do.

In comprehending this noble effort we are making, it's important that you understand *why* we want diversity. One reason we want diversity is because this is America, we are a melting pot, where everyone is guaranteed, as someone famous once put it, "Life, liberty and the pursuit of happiness."

Another reason we want diversity is because we in the legal profession are honor bound to uphold the rule of law and the ideal of justice. And justice, as you know if you're at all familiar with the lady in the Statue of Liberty (which was given to us by France, a very nice gift), is blind.

And another reason we want diversity is this: If we

don't start getting a few of Those People into our firm, it's going to knock the hell out of our business. Those People are starting to control some major clients and governmental entities, none of whom are going to give our firm a nickel of business pretty soon. Not that we are motivated in our diversity efforts by crass economic considerations like that or anything.

To kick off our renewed effort to achieve greater diversity within the firm (which has always been a big priority with us, even though we've never thought or said much about it before), I am proud to announce that the diversity committee has declared 1995 to be The Year of the Diverse Person at Fairweather, Winters & Sommers. Furthermore, it has adopted the following resolution: "We at Fairweather, Winters & Sommers love everybody who's different than us."

But talk is cheap. The real question is what action are we at the Fairweather firm taking to promote diversity. Well, here are a few things we're doing, just to show you how serious we are about this effort.

Studies have shown that one of the reasons that minorities do not succeed in law firms is the lack of role models. Since the Fairweather firm does not have minority role models, we have gone that extra step and hired twenty role models from Those People Role Modeling International, a firm that specializes in providing diverse role models to businesses.

To create an area in which minorities are sure to feel comfortable in our firm, we have established—on an interim basis—a minority department. This department will be staffed entirely by minority attorneys and support staff, and will serve only minority clients. To avoid any possible friction with other departments within the firm, the minority department will be housed—on an interim basis—in a separate building. We, of course, have no intention of segregating our minority lawyers. This separation is merely an interim measure which we hope to phase out as soon as we can train our Neanderthal partners to exhibit a little sensitivity.

I'd also like to announce that the firm has instituted sensitivity training for our Neanderthal partners. As part of this effort, the firm has outlawed all ethnic jokes, except those that are really funny and would be offensive only to somebody who was uptight and supersensitive, and so would never succeed at this firm anyway. Much of what gets in the way of better relations between different groups is innocent misunderstandings. We believe that through education we can strip away this veneer of innocent misunderstanding and get to the core of intentional vicious behavior.

The first diversity training session, which was held last week, showed that there's room left for improvement. Lawyers attending the session were asked to role play the parts of different ethnic groups in trying to resolve a sensitive issue. Unfortunately, the session degenerated into a race riot composed entirely of white anglo-saxon protestant men. The sensitivity group leader was forced to call in Chief Fitzpatrick of the Fairweather security force to quell the disturbance.

Another effort we are undertaking revolves around getting our lawyers more in tune with different cultural and ethnic groups around the world. Each month, we are going to pick a different country and study the geography, politics, history, and culture of that country. This will culminate each month in a party with the music, folkdancing, and food of the country, in which all of our lawyers will come dressed up in costumes appropriate to the country. We have hired a fourth-grade teacher from a local elementary school to lead these units.

Finally, I have begun a personal grassroots campaign

to start a dialogue with Those People, which some of you may wish to emulate. When I run into a minority anyplace, I just stop him or her and say, "Hi, I'm Phillip D. W. Wilson III and I'm looking to achieve diversity." Then I establish rapport by talking to them about what interests me, you know, polo, the stock market and the like. And finally I try to get them to open up to me, talk to me about how it feels to be a minority, do they feel oppressed, things like that. So far, I would have to say this has mainly gotten me a lot of stares. But I'm going to keep at it, because I know that diversity will not be achieved overnight. And we at Fairweather, Winters & Sommers are in this diversity thing for the long haul.

Together, brothers and sisters, I know that we shall overcome.

Pause for Applause

THE FOLLOWING SPEECH was written by Lieutenant Colonel Clinton L. Hargraves, CPA for delivery to the 1994 annual meeting of the National Association of Law Firm Administrators held in Philadelphia on June 30, 1994.

Thank you kindly for that most generous and gracious introduction. Ladies and gentlemen, honored guests, and assorted celebrities, I am truly humbled at the honor bestowed upon me in being asked to fulfill the keynote address function for this fine association at this significant meeting. I do not feel worthy of such an honor, but then who am I to quibble with the keynote address committee, which chose me, above all others, to execute the keynote address-giving responsibility. No, certainly I am not going to impugn their fine reputations by suggesting that they have selected somebody who is unworthy of this honor. Instead, I'll just do my goshdarndest to deliver to you a rip-roaring keynote speech that, to quote one of our great American presidents a bit out of context, you will "long remember." And, if I may quote that same president a bit further, it is "altogether fitting and proper" that our fine association be meeting here in this historic city on the brink of another Fourth of July celebrating the independence of this great nation of ours in whose military I served proudly for many years. [Pause for applause.]

Yes, as we approach the year 2000, the twenty-first century—by the way, don't you think it's a little confusing how when we reach the twenty-first century we'll only be into the two thousands in years, but I guess that's how it's

always been, except in the B.C.s, so we'd best get used to
it. Anyway, as I was saying, as we approach both the
Fourth of July and the twenty-first century, I think that
this is an appropriate time for us at the National Association of Law Firm Administrators here at our annual meeting in Philadelphia to reflect, to ask ourselves the
question, where have we been? Where are we now? Where
are we going? How will we get there? When will we get
there? What are the roadblocks? How do we get around
those roadblocks? What happens if something unexpected
happens? What do we do then? It is questions such as
these that I would like to address for you today in this
keynote speech. [Take sip of water and smile out at the
audience, making eye contact with several people.]

That reminds me of a little story. This fellow—
actually maybe it could be a lady, let's make it a lady, no
sexism here—this lady walks into a bar, reaches into her
pocket, and takes out this tiny donkey which she puts on
the bar and says to the bartender, "Bartender . . ." No,
now that I think about it, it really does have to be a
fellow. And I probably shouldn't tell this joke here. But it's
one hell of a cute joke, so if you're interested, please come
and see me after this keynote address.

But enough levity. Where was I, oh yes, where have
we been, where are we going, etc.

Well, we've come from a place where we didn't exist.
Now that may seem strange, but what is it they say about
truth, that it's often stranger than fiction? How true. Yes,
strange as it seems—especially to those of us here at this
annual meeting of the National Association of Law Firm
Administrators in Philadelphia—law firms existed without
us for well over a century. How did they manage to do
that? Well, don't ask me.

Of course, law firms were much smaller back then. If
you had a firm of say one or two lawyers, I suppose you

didn't really need a firm administrator, or at least not an administrator of the top-notch caliber of the people in this particular room—I believe it's called the Crystal Ballroom—at this annual meeting of the National Association of Law Firm Administrators at which I am delivering this keynote address.

Gradually, of course, as firms grew they came to realize how badly they needed us and they hired us in droves. At first they hired us to do little menial things, like prepare and oversee the firm budget, collect receivables and the like. But gradually, we've worked our way up into positions of real power that involve serving on firm committees, circulating memos announcing the promotion of staff members, and being invited to the lawyers' summer party.

Which brings us to where we are now. As a military man, I'm tempted to analogize our position as firm administrators to that of generals. (I never made general myself in the military. Got passed over several times, for political reasons. But that was long ago and we're not here to rehash that unfortunate occurrence.) Of course, I acknowledge that the partner in our firm is President, Commander-in-Chief, as it were. In fact, we've got a lot of presidents and commanders-in-chief in our firms, don't we? Okay, so the analogy isn't perfect.

But anyway, we're the ones out there on the front lines, and in the trenches. So maybe we're not the generals after all, say we're majors or corporals. And so that's where we are now, the way that I see it.

Where are we going? you ask me. Good question. The way I see it, if we keep our eyes on the ball and our noses clean, stay on the straight and narrow, with our ears to the ground and our mouths pretty well shut (since loose lips sink ships), I'd say we've got nowhere to go but up. But if we take our eyes off the ball, let our noses get dirty, etc., we, the National Association of Law Firm Administrators, both as a group and individually, could be in very serious trouble.

But if we've got nowhere to go but up, how do we get there? I say we just plunge on, damn the torpedoes, full speed ahead, go for it. More positions on more firm committees, larger offices with better views, more assistants and staff, letterhead with our names and phone numbers printed on it, our very own fax machines right in our offices—the sky's the limit. But of course, we can't plunge on blindly. We have got to plan. And I say that nobody, but nobody, is better equipped to plan than we law firm administrators. [Pause for applause] Wasn't it Franklin Roosevelt who said, "We have nothing to fear but fear itself?" Well he was right, by golly. [Sip water, smile, make more eye contact.]

Now what do I see as the major roadblocks to continued growth in our organization and in our individual capacities? Speaking candidly, I see quite a number of things that could derail us. Incompetency would be one. Ignorance would be another. Still another would be greed. Dishonesty wouldn't be good, either. And neither would coveting thy neighbor's wife.

Now I don't say for a second that any of you have these faults. In fact, I hope to heck that none of you do. But it doesn't do you any good to stick your head in the sand, does it? Not a bit. You've got to face up to it. Wasn't it Harry Truman who said, "The buck stops here"?

I wish time permitted me to cover all the other interesting and significant issues I raised at the beginning of my keynote address, but I see by the old clock on the wall that I'd better be heading into my wrap-up. Of course, if I should be invited back next year, I'd be happy to address some of those other issues.

In closing, I'd like to leave you with these two

thoughts, both of which have been said before by somebody famous:

"It's an ill wind that blows no good."

And "You can fool many of the people some of the time, and others at other times, but you can't fool a majority of the people regularly, day in and day out."

Good morning, and God bless you all, you're a wonderful audience.

[EDITOR'S NOTE: Unfortunately, this speech was never delivered by Clint, since he was not asked to be the keynote speaker. Clint is not sorry to have composed this speech, however, since he feels it will be equally poignant any time in the next five years and thereafter, with only minor modifications to his references to the twenty-first century.]

Promoting Your Boss

by Bertha Oxenhandle

MR. FAIRWEATHER asked me to contribute to this book. I protested that I'm no writer, and besides, I'm not a lawyer (after 35 years as his secretary, he probably realized that).

He told me that this was going to be a book mainly by the staff, that the heads of our departments were each going to write a chapter. I told him that I was not the head of any department, that he should get our secretarial supervisor to do a piece.

He said that I was the head of him. I told him that he was no department.

He said that this book could help future generations of support staff at law firms by giving them some hints on how to survive. Here he had me. I figure if I can help somebody avoid some of my mistakes, I ought to give it a try, whether I can write or not. So here they are, for the first time anywhere . . .

BERTHA'S TEN RULES FOR LEGAL SECRETARY SUCCESS

Rule Number One. Keep your ears open. If you do, you can learn a lot that will help your boss. Particularly if he's a partner, the poor fella's not going to have the foggiest notion of what the heck's going on around the firm. You, on the other hand, can learn practically everything that's going on, just by listening to people talk—while you wait in line to use the photocopy machine, in elevators, in the washroom, in the staff coffee room, etc.

Rule Number Two. Keep your mouth shut. Did you know that secretary in some language or another means one who keeps secrets? All of the things you will be learning by keeping your ears open are being said by people to show how "in" they are on what's going on, or to gossip. Much of what you hear is likely to get lawyers of other secretaries who do not keep their mouths shut in trouble. If you talk too much, sooner or later you are going to say something (quite innocently, I'm sure) that gets your boss in trouble, and he's going to figure out where the leak is coming from—and plug you. (The only thing I worry about is that if everyone followed this rule, sources of information would dry up completely, and life around the law firm would get awfully dull. Given what I've learned about human nature in my many years on this planet, though, I'm not going to worry too much about that happening.)

Rule Number Three. Admit your mistakes readily. No matter how good you are, you'll make plenty of them. And even when something's not your fault, you may want to take responsibility. Put yourself in your boss's place. Which would you rather hear in response to "Bertha, Joe Turner just called and said that the document that was to have been sent with my letter to him the other day was not enclosed."

A. "I'm sorry, Mr. Fairweather, I must have forgotten. I'll send a copy out right away."

B. "You never told me to send him a copy of that document."

C. "I'm sure I enclosed it; our mailroom probably didn't seal the envelope correctly, and so the document must have fallen out in the mail."

D. "Mr. Turner's secretary must have misplaced it,

but I guess I'll send them another one, if you want me to."

E. "Big deal. Mr. Turner never reads the documents we send him anyway."

Rule Number Four. Treat everyone kindly, and with respect. You may think that lawyers around the firm are important to you, but the support staff is going to be a whole lot more important in getting your work done. For example, our duplicating, word-processing, and messenger departments are always very busy. So when you need a special favor done for your boss, who's more likely to do it for you—the support person who you've just treated like a mongrel, or the person you've just chatted with and thanked for the nice job they did for you the other day?

Rule Number Five. When you can't get something done in the time your boss expects it, let him know as soon as possible. There's a story told about how Nails Nuttree, head of our litigation department, once reacted to a secretary of his who failed to follow that rule. First time the secretary left at 5 o'clock without completing something Nails had told him he needed to get out that day, Nails told him that if he ever surprised him like that again, he'd have a little surprise for him. A few weeks later the secretary did the same thing. When he returned to the office the following morning, he found somebody sitting in his desk chair who handed him an envelope that contained a final check and a note from Nails that said, "In baseball, it's three strikes and you're out. With Nails, it's two. Nails"

Rule Number Six. Don't tell your boss he's wrong. He will be, just don't tell him. One thing about lawyers is that they generally recognize a stupid mistake when they've made one. (They have quite a lot of practice.) Tell them about their mistake, and they get angry at *you*. But correct it for them without calling it a mistake, and you're a hero.

Rule Number Seven. Learn to recognize clients' voices, and call them by name. Most of lawyering is making clients feel that they are valued and important. You can help your boss achieve that simply by calling his clients by name. And you can add to a client's impression that he is important by telling him that you'll be sure that [the lawyer you work for] gets his message as soon as possible, or that [your lawyer] will be sorry to have missed his call, or you're sure [your lawyer] will get right back to him. Of course, when your lawyer doesn't return the call, all of your good work will have gone for naught. I guess there are some things you just can't control.

Rule Number Eight. Do not date lawyers at your firm. To phrase it mathematically, love plus work equals big trouble. I know what a powerful force love is. But think about it, there are probably about 150 million people in this country of whatever sex your preference may lean towards who are not lawyers in your firm. Don't you suppose that you might find one or two people in that category who could fit your bill?

Rule Number Nine. Don't flaunt your knowledge of the law. By the time you are a secretary at the firm for two or three years, you will know much more about the practice of law than most young associates (and many partners). It is best to continue to feign ignorance, however, for two reasons. First, it pisses lawyers off to discover that secretaries know more about the practice of law than they do. [EDITOR'S NOTE: Bertha had written "may tend to anger lawyers," but Stanley changed it to "pisses lawyers off." Bertha threatened to withdraw permission to use her piece unless this note was inserted.] Second, if you let on how much you know, lawyers will be pestering you constantly for legal advice, which makes it very difficult to get your secretarial work done.

Rule Number Ten. Pretend that your boss is the boss. You and he both know that he is far more dispensable than you. Let that remain unspoken. Lawyers like to think that they are in control. As long as they don't get too far out of line, let it pass. You have much more important things to worry about than who's called the boss.

* * *

So those are Bertha's ten rules. If you follow them, you too may wind up being secretary to somebody like Mr. Fairweather for thirty-five years. That may sound like a frightening prospect, but I wouldn't trade it for anything.

Now, of course, most of my rules are just plain common sense. I know that. But one thing a secretary picks up pretty quickly, if she keeps her eyes and ears open, is just how uncommon common sense is.

We Give at the Office

by Orville Figuremeister

BEFORE I ARRIVED at the firm as comptroller, charitable and political contributions at Fairweather, Winters & Sommers were made on an ad hoc basis. Whenever a Fairweather partner wanted to make a contribution, he or she simply directed our bookkeeping department to issue a check. In my annual review of the firm's finances four years ago, I suggested to the Executive Committee that they try to bring greater rationality to contribution decisions—and save the firm some money. The EC plunged into action immediately, creating the Committee on Political and Charitable Contributions and making me an ex officio member. Here is a transcript of a meeting of that committee that took place some three years ago.

"I say we give them fifty bucks."

"Give who?"

"Make it a hundred."

"Who are we talking about?"

"I'll see your hundred, and raise it to two."

"Could somebody please tell me . . ."

"Let's go to two-fifty."

"Wait a minute, this sounds more like an auction than thoughtful deliberation. Remember, we were created to avoid willy-nilly contributions."

"Why should we discriminate against him?"

"Discriminate against who?"

"Willy Nilly—isn't he running for county recorder of deeds?"

"No, that's Willie Wilson."

"Oh."

"Why don't we give him a hundred bucks."

"Who?"

"Willie Nelson. And we ought to give his opponent a hundred, too."

"Why?"

"It's only fair."

"What's fair got to do with it?"

"Look, can we slow down a minute. I think we need to approach this more logically. Why are we making these charitable and political contributions in the first place?"

"Good question."

"I'll bite, why are we?"

"I don't think we can lump charitable and political contributions together. Why don't we separate them out and talk about them one at a time?"

"I'd rather lump them."

"I'll lump you."

"Now now, let's try to act civil to one another."

"OK, let's take charitable contributions first. Why do we make them?"

"That's easy. Because we're a generous, public-spirited group that is naturally interested in giving all of our money away to good causes."

"Don't be sarcastic. Anyway, there are hundreds of equally good causes that we don't give money to, so it must be something more than just that."

"Well, don't we give to charities that are law-related?"

"Sometimes. We support the local legal aid office and a couple of public interest law firms, but we also gave money to the Victory Gardens Theater Company, which is not exactly law-related."

"Yes, but Lionel Hartz's wife is on the board of that company, so that's why we contributed."

"And that's the same principle, I suppose, that caused us to take a quarter-page ad in Alphonse Proust's daughter Suzy's high school yearbook."

"No, I think Alphonse argued that that was for business development, since those high schoolers may grow up to be clients one of these days."

"But what about the Triple P, why did we give to them?"

"The Triple P?"

"Yes, the Society for the Preservation of Polo Ponies."

"Don't tell me we contributed to that."

"Of course we did. That's the favorite charity of Byron Fair, chairman of Stanley's client Fair Toxi-Beaut Corporation."

"Oh yeah, I forgot."

"What about law schools? I know we contribute a lot of money to them."

"I guess that falls into law-related. And we should give them something because, after all, they do provide us all of our cannon fodder—I mean, new associates."

"So maybe the common thread is that it's law-related, spouse-on-the-board, client-pet-project charities that we contribute to."

"No, there are general funds too, like the Community Chest."

"Yes, come to think of it, I've always wondered why we contribute to the Community Chest. I mean it's a good cause and all, but why do we contribute to them as a firm?"

"Blackmail."

"What do you mean, blackmail?"

"Well, the Community Chest has a big annual fundraiser and in the program booklet they list all of the law firms that have contributed. It would be unseemly for us not to appear on that list as at least a Benefactor.

Besides, the fundraising chair of that group is always the president of some corporation we're trying to land as a client."

"I've always wondered how we decide how much to contribute to these different charities."

"That's easy, we just contribute the same amount we did last year."

"But how did we decide to contribute *that* amount?"

"Gosh, you don't understand anything, do you. We arrive at that amount scientifically, because it's the amount we contributed the year before that."

"But what if we didn't contribute last year? How do we decide how much to contribute to a new charitable organization?"

"We try to avoid new charities on the ground that we're cutting back."

"No, we're not 'cutting back,' we're 'focusing our charitable giving on a few charities, where it can do the most good.'"

"Oh yes, focusing, I forgot."

"But when we're forced to contribute, how much do we give?"

"We used to have a formula that tied the amount of the contribution to a percentage of the annual billing of the person proposing the contribution, but that started producing contributions that were too generous."

"So why didn't we just reduce the percentage?"

"Nobody thought of that."

"Or just match the amount that the partner contributed personally?"

"No, we didn't want to do that; that would have eliminated our firm contributions entirely."

"So how do we determine the amount of our contributions now?"

"Well, usually we argue about it for quite a while,

until eventually we decide on the lowest amount we can contribute without appearing to be unduly chintzy."

"We have to move this discussion along. It's almost time to adjourn and we haven't even begun to talk about political contributions."

"Yes we have, what about Willie Nelson?"

"Wilson. I mean we haven't talked about the *principles* of political giving."

"Sure we have. When you think about it, they're pretty much the same principles as we apply to charitable giving, aren't they?"

"What do you mean?"

"Well, we give to good candidates, to candidates supported by members of our lawyers' families or by clients, to candidates we're blackmailed into supporting and so forth. And the amount we give is pretty much the same as our charitable giving—the lowest amount that's not too chintzy."

"In other words, we give pretty much to whoever our partners say we should, and there's no way around that. Doesn't sound like our committee is going to save the firm much money, does it?"

"Well, there is one way we could save the firm some money, in the long run."

"I'll bet I know what you're going to suggest—adopt a rule that there will be no firm contributions?"

"No, the firm would never accept that, not yet. Our contribution policy is too much a part of firm culture."

"Well, what are you getting at, saying 'in the long run' and 'not yet'?"

"The way I see it, the reason the firm tolerates our charitable and political giving is that we're so chintzy it hardly costs the firm anything. If we really want to reduce costs we've got to recommend that the firm increase its charitable and political giving three- or four-fold. Then the

cost of the program will be so large, the Executive
Committee will be forced to act. And since there's no way
of rationally limiting our charitable and political giving,
they'll just wipe it out altogether, which will save us all a
bunch of money in the long run."

*   *   *

The committee was prescient. The year after establishing
its more generous giving policy, firm contributions quadrupled. When I pointed out that increase to the Executive
Committee, they circulated this terse memo to all lawyers:

"Because the firm does not want to deprive its lawyers of the joy of personally contributing to charities and
political candidates of their choice, the firm will no longer
make any contributions. The Executive Committee also
wishes to thank the members of the Committee on
Political and Charitable Contributions for their excellent
services, which will no longer be needed."

Me, I got a nice raise for reducing our contribution
expenses to zero. It just goes to show you—sometimes
you've got to spend a buck to save a buck.

Revolting Developments

PRIOR TO THE TIME that Chief Brian Fitzpatrick signed on at the Fairweather firm to head its security operation, the firm suffered an unfortunate incident which led temporarily to the resignation of the entire Executive Committee. In an effort to study the incident and prevent any recurrence, Chief Fitzpatrick investigated and assembled the following hour-by-hour account of what happened:

December 22, 1987, 11 P.M. After work, Fairweather, Winters & Sommers associates congregate in the firm library to plan the traditional associates' skit for the firm's Christmas party.

December 23, 1987, 12:30 A.M. Associates develop ideas for four vignettes. Vignette one, using a chain-gang motif, spoofs how associates at Fairweather, Winters & Sommers work an average of 2,500 billable hours each year while partners bill only 1,200. Vignette two, set on a plantation in pre-Civil War Alabama, pokes fun at how the partners make 14 times what associates make. Vignette three takes place in a house of ill repute. It makes light of how the average divorce rate among associates in the first two years at the firm was 50 percent (52 percent of FW&S associates were married). Vignette four satirizes the economic problems that had caused the firm not to make any new partners in the last 13 years.

December 23, 1987, 4:00 A.M. Scripts for all vignettes written and rehearsed. Associate Harry Slatkin suggests that maybe the whole thing isn't so funny. According to one associate at the party, Ralph Frontz (who asked not to be named), Slatkin had been drinking heavily and had the reputation among the associates of being a wimp and a complainer: definitely partnership material.

December 23, 1987, 4:22 A.M. Sarah B. Little points out to Harry that the firm has made great strides in recent years on matters of associate rights. Slatkin argues that this is so much window dressing: when it comes to calling the shots, the partners and only the partners count.

December 23, 1987, 5:00 A.M. Other associates move to Slatkin's point of view. An Associates Revolutionary Committee ("ARC") is formed. Loretta Freebisch-Hart, a Harvard Law School graduate and former research assistant to Professor Duncan X, is elected chair. Sarah Little resigns from associates' skit committee, leaves meeting.

December 23, 1987, 5:10 A.M. Committee decides, regretfully, that the only course available to them is to assume complete control of the firm. Freebisch-Hart cautions that given the vested interests of the reactionary junta in power—the so-called Executive Committee—it is evident that control will come neither easily nor peaceably. She quotes Professor X, who said in his recent law review article that "the revolution will come when we gain control over the Xerox machines at Cravath, Swaine & Moore."

December 23, 1987, 7:15 A.M. ARC continues to explore alternative methods for gaining control; begins work on World Associate Revolutionary Manifesto. Members debate whether they should utilize the current Executive Committee's method of assuming power—identifying key firm clients and informing them that the senior partners who had serviced their needs well for 40 years had suddenly become senile and that henceforth a new group would tend to their needs.

December 23, 1987, 9:15 A.M. Sarah Little delivers handwritten memo to word processing, and requests rush status. Memo, which warns Executive Committee of possible ARC takeover, remains untyped until January 14, 1988 because Nails Nuttree's law review article takes precedence.

December 23, 1987, 10:20 A.M. ARC decides that the jealous control the E.C. keeps over their recently stolen clients makes their plan impractical, unless ARC takes over control of the firm's communication network. That option is rejected because none of the associates can even understand the firm's telephone manual.

December 23, 1987, 1:15 P.M. ARC reportedly considers a scheme for physically capturing FW&S partners and holding them prisoner until they agree to relinquish power, but abandons the plan, fearing potential liability for false imprisonment. More important than the liability is their concern that the captured partners might hold out for several days before surrendering, forcing ARC associates to spend days with people whose company for even a few minutes they find unbearable. The group phones Professor X at Harvard to seek advice. He says, "Advice? Don't ask me. I'm a law professor. I just talk and write. Action is way out of my realm."

December 23, 1987, 4:25 P.M. Lisle Goodfellow III submits plan for a small group to steal into the firm in the dead of night, break into the accounting department, and assume control of the firm's accounting records. Goodfellow's plan is voted down because the partnership maintains back-up records of its financial dealings. At worst, Goodfellow's proposal might cause partnership temporary inconvenience and minor expense. Not worth the risk. Something more devastating must be found.

December 24, 1987, 4:00 P.M. Christmas party goes off as scheduled. Associate skits are a big hit, although, as usual, several partners complain that they "don't get it."

December 26, 1987, 2:10 A.M. Lottie Freebisch-Hart

proposes they adopt Professor X's quip and turn it into reality. Associates will strike at the very nerve center of the firm, seize control of it and, from there, hold the work-product of the entire firm hostage. Manifesto drafting committee reports work is progressing slowly.

December 27, 1987, 9:47 A.M. Disguised as repairmen, three members of ARC make their way into the firm's duplicating department, brandish firearms, and seize control of the Xerox machines.

December 27, 1987, 10:00 A.M. Over the paging system, Lottie broadcasts the following message: "Hello. This is Comrade Loretta Freebisch-Hart of the Associates Revolutionary Committee. At 9:47 this morning we took control of the central duplicating facilities. There were no casualties. Please remain calm and do as we say, and no one will be hurt. We repeat, 'Do as we say and no one will be hurt.'"

December 27, 1987, 10:15 A.M. Lottie pages, demanding that Executive Committee member Stephen Falderall report to central duplicating facilities to meet with ARC. Falderall reports and is told by ARC that he and his partners should expect to experience a slowdown in service out of the firm duplicating department. Falderall says he understands, and asks what ARC is demanding. ARC tells Falderall it needs total control of the firm. Falderall chuckles and says the firm can survive a slowdown in duplicating services, especially since service is so slow now it is unlikely anybody would notice. Falderall is right.

December 27, 1987, 1:25 P.M. Sarah Little forms Loyal Associates Counter-revolutionary Committee ("LACC"), which pledges allegiance to Executive Committee and claims ARC does not speak for the majority of associates.

December 27, 1987, 2:20 P.M. ARC tells LACC it

doesn't care who speaks for the majority of associates, as long as they have control of duplicating.

December 27, 1987, 10:00 P.M. ARC orders bunkbeds moved from library into duplicating room. Samantha Priddy, firm librarian, tries to prevent the removal of the beds, pointing to rules regarding bed removal posted in the library. Ms. Priddy is gagged and bound to the CCH Federal Tax Reporter stack.

December 27, 1987, 11:00 P.M. Firm messengers deliver dinner from Chef Effete's restaurant, Tail of the Pig. Several associates send the meal back, claiming lamb is underdone. Chef Effete is furious and sends back message, "If you do not like zee lamb, zen go to zee Golden Arches." ARC occupation forces settle in for the night with Big Macs and fries.

December 28, 1987, 10:00 A.M. Subcommittee of LACC cuts Ms. Priddy loose from CCH stacks.

December 28, 1987, 11:45 A.M. Falderall is again summoned to a meeting with ARC and told that, commencing immediately, the duplicating department will decline to staple documents. Falderall says he is willing to consider reasonable requests ARC might make and suggests that his partners might be convinced to give ARC a seat on the Executive Committee. Lottie tells Falderall that ARC does not recognize the Executive Committee as a legitimate power in the firm, and hence Falderall's proposal is totally unacceptable. Manifesto committee tries out several slogan ideas on ARC members; adopts "Associates of the world, unite; you have nothing to lose but your billable hours."

December 28, 1987, 8:00 P.M. Fresh reinforcements are brought in by the revolutionary committee to hold duplicating room for the night. Fearing a counter-attack by LACC, ARC occupation force goes through maneuvers, feeding documents at random to the firm paper shredder and brandishing razor-sharp staple removers at passersby. LACC moves file cabinets in front of duplicating room to try to block ingress and egress.

Next two days. Over the next two days, the seriousness of the situation escalates. ARC announces that it is going to remove page 6 from all documents it duplicates. LACC develops plan to have word processing produce a meaningless page 6 for all documents, but lawyers have difficulty distinguishing a meaningful page 6 from a meaningless page 6. ARC decides to remove pages at random. Falderall offers ARC two seats on the Executive Committee. Finally, ARC's threat to switch pages between documents, coupled with plans uncovered by the partnership for an ARC attack on word processing, brings the Executive Committee to its knees and leads to mass resignations.

December 31, 1987, 1:00 P.M. ARC declares itself in control, replacing the Executive Committee with the Supreme Soviet of Working Lawyers. Manifesto fails to be adopted, 4-1; sent back to committee for further work.

January 7, 1988. Associates, having examined all firm financial records and having experienced running the firm for one week, return all power to the Executive Committee, concluding that they want no part of managing this place. ARC and LACC dissolve.

* * *

After studying the above account, Chief Fitzpatrick ordered immediate steps designed to ensure that no future associate uprising would develop. He circulated a memo announcing, "After consultin' with Mr. Fairweather, it's da official firm policy dat dere'll be no more associate skits at firm Christmas parties, henceforth."

Time, For a Change

by Adam Nieve

I'LL BE BRIEF. Time's my business. Managing it. Saving it. They say time flies. Maybe so. Maybe not. I'm no philosopher. Never have been. Never will. I just manage time. My time. Others' time.

This driving you nuts? Short sentences. No fluff. Hemingway. Helps move things along. It's direct. And around the bush is someplace I don't like to beat.

But I've found that talking like this drives people crazy, so I'll switch to longer sentences, in the interest of education.

Look, I used to waste time just like everyone else. Then one day, I woke up and said to myself, "Adam, your life is slipping away."

"What do you mean by that?" I asked myself.

"We're only given so many days on this good round earth, Adam m'boy," I answered kindly. "And you're not using yours to the fullest."

"What do you mean by that?" I again asked myself.

"You go from one thing to the next, Adam, then back to the first, on to the third, back to the second, over to the fourth, back to the first. You've got no rhyme, no reason, no flow, no organization. You go hither and yon, then hither again."

"I'm still not sure I catch your drift," I admitted reluctantly.

"Look, Adam, we've already wasted fifteen minutes

and made no discernible progress. This has got to stop," I answered.

Well, that conversation proved to be a turning point in my life. I began to take control of my own time, began walking myself through my days, seeing exactly where and how I was wasting time and how I could avoid doing that.

In the process, I became an expert. And now I do for the lawyers and staff at the Fairweather firm what I used to do for myself. I walk them through their days.

Let me explain how this walking works. I'll take the example of Geodfrey A. Bleschieu, with whom I did some work recently. In order to really help people, I need to live with them. So I moved in with Geodfrey and Rebecca Bleschieu. At first, they thought having me on a cot in their bedroom was a bit of an imposition, but after a while they got so used to me they hardly knew I was there. Here is a description of a recent day I spent with Geodfrey.

Alarm clock goes off at 6:00 A.M. I shout over to Rebecca to hit the snooze alarm to give us ten more minutes of shut-eye.

At 6:10 A.M. Geodfrey, Becky and I arise. My turn to use the washroom first and I'm out by 6:20, since I've laid out my razor, shaving cream and toothbrush (with toothpaste on it) the night before. Geodfrey and Becky finish in the washroom and we meet in the kitchen for a quick breakfast. I have trained Geodfrey to put out the cereal in bowls the night before and to set the automatic coffeemaker.

Geodfrey grabs the sports section and is distressed to read about the Bulls' heart-breaking loss to the Knicks, in double overtime. While Geodfrey is reading the sports section, I skim three business magazines, dictate notes on six key articles, check my appointment schedule, read the

Wall Street Journal and leave a voice mail for my stock-broker.

By 7 A.M. Geodfrey and I are out the door, having both kissed Becky good-bye (on opposite cheeks, at the same time). We hop into the car and Geodfrey drives to the office at five miles below the speed limit. By 7:15 we are back at Geodfrey's house, since he has forgotten to take his briefcase and overnight bag.

By 7:30 we are inside the office building. Geodfrey has decided to come in early in order to work on a major project. He is leaving the office at 4 P.M. to fly to New York for a crucial negotiation session in this matter. Geodfrey has not been able to work on the matter since it arose, six months ago, because he's been pretty swamped.

Geodfrey and I get on the elevator with Chris, a senior associate at the firm. Chris says he would like to meet later that day to get Geodfrey's advice, since Chris is preparing a brief in a matter which has issues similar to those Geodfrey dealt with in another case.

Geodfrey opens his briefcase to reach for the day's calendar, dumping the contents of the briefcase onto the elevator floor. When we arrive at Chris's floor, Geodfrey has Chris press the elevator hold button while he gathers up the rest of his materials and stuffs them into his brief-case. Geodfrey suggests that they meet in Chris's office at 10:30.

After stepping out of the elevator, Geodfrey decides to run down to the mailroom to see if the latest issue of *Sports Illustrated* (the swimsuit issue) has arrived. It has. Geodfrey passes a coffee room and stops for a cup of coffee to take back to his desk to get him going. In the coffee room Geodfrey gets into a fifteen-minute discussion about the Bulls-Knicks game with Ellen Jane Ritton, an obnoxious New Yorker and ardent Knicks fan.

Striding down the hall towards his office, Geodfrey

leafs through his *Sports Illustrated* and crashes into Gary Swath, scalding Swath with his coffee. Swath picks himself up from the carpet and asks Geodfrey for advice on handling a litigation matter. Geodfrey says, "Sure, call me later. But, you know, wait a second, I think a case just came down from the Supreme Court a few weeks ago. Let's go to the library and see if we can find it in the advance sheets." Geodfrey and Gary go into the library where, in half an hour, they are able to find the Supreme Court case that Geodfrey was thinking of, which has no bearing whatsoever on Gary's case.

Geodfrey makes it into his office and realizes he has forgotten his *Sports Illustrated* in the library. He returns to retrieve it and has to fight to wrest it away from two young male associates who have an intense interest in this year's swim gear.

Back in his office, Geodfrey finds that his E-mail contains two messages from Garrison M. Phelps, with whom Geodfrey is working on another major matter. Garrison wants to see Geodfrey right away. Geodfrey walks over to Garrison's office, but Garrison is out.

Back in his office, Geodfrey begins returning phone calls from the stack of phone messages on his desk. Many of those people are not in now, so Geodfrey leaves messages. Geodfrey forgets all about the 10:30 meeting with Chris and has to reschedule it for the afternoon. Geodfrey reviews the morning's mail and dictates responses for his secretary to type.

Geodfrey decides that he needs a little break and walks down to the coffee room, where he meets two lawyers he has been working with on another important matter. They get into a heated discussion, but finally arrive at a consensus—that B. J. Armstrong definitely was fouled on the final shot of last night's Bulls-Knicks game.

On the way back to his office, Geodfrey stops at

Garrison's office, where Garrison is on a phone call. Geodfrey sits down to wait for Garrison and wads up pieces of paper from Garrison's desk to shoot at Garrison's waste basketball net. Geodfrey hits three of five shots. Garrison finishes his phone call and says that he has forgotten what it was he wanted to talk to Geodfrey about, but they do spend twenty minutes discussing a partnership memorandum concerning compensation. Geodfrey tells Garrison that he wishes Garrison had not wadded up pages from the original will of Geodfrey's dying aunt for his waste basketball shots. Garrison retrieves the sheets and promises that when he returns from his business trip he will iron them so they'll look like new.

Geodfrey returns to his office, consumes a sandwich at his desk and begins preparing notes for the negotiation session in New York. Pat, a senior associate in Geodfrey's department, drops by Geodfrey's office to ask "a quick question that just came up on a very important matter" for a project for Geodfrey's biggest client, which Pat has been handling alone. Pat spends ten minutes laying out the background of the matter, and Geodfrey answers the question, which was a matter of common sense that any idiot would have figured out in less than a minute.

Getting back to preparing for the meeting, Geodfrey can't seem to remember the previous history of the negotiations. He reviews the file for another twenty-five minutes, then Chris comes in for their rescheduled meeting.

Geodfrey's secretary interrupts their conference to say that Geodfrey has been asked to attend a practice group meeting dealing with the training needs of associates. When that meeting finishes an hour later, Geodfrey returns telephone calls to people who have returned his calls, then revises the drafts of correspondence he dictated earlier.

Geodfrey realizes that it will be time to leave for the

airport in twenty minutes, so he asks me to call Rebecca to say good-bye, while he goes down to the bookstore in the basement of the building to pick up "a trashy novel for the plane." Exhausted, Geodfrey and I head for the airport, but get caught up in traffic and miss our plane to New York.

To help Geodfrey with his time management, I review my notes of the day with him and we spend the next seven hours discussing what he might do differently to use his time more effectively. Together we come up with the following solutions:

1. Rewire the snooze alarm, so that when Becky hits it, the radio will stay on and the volume level will double.

2. Pour milk in the cereal the night before (so what if it's a little soggy).

3. Drive to work at seven miles over the speed limit.

4. Never read the sports section; it's too aggravating, anyway.

5. Upon entering an elevator and noticing that someone from the firm is in it, press the emergency stop button and vacate immediately.

6. Cancel the *Sports Illustrated* subscription, and substitute the *American Bar Association Journal,* which, mercifully, has no swimsuit issue.

7. Buy a small coffeemaker for Geodfrey's office.

8. Ignore E-mail and phone calls; if it's that damn important, they'll call back.

9. Fire Pat.

10. Forget about continuing legal education for associates on the theory that, "I got along without it, so can they, especially with what we pay them."

11. Get an associate to handle the New York negotiation.

*   *   *

I'd love to dwell on the basis for our analysis longer, but I've got to run and pack. Tomorrow I move in with Fawn Plush and her husband, Hannibal.

Confidentially Speaking

by T. William Williams

IN THE COURSE of our firm's work, both our legal and support staff come into possession of some top-secret information about our clients, which is susceptible to abuse. I first became aware of that susceptibility the time three members of our messenger staff bought BMWs and left the firm suddenly to retire on the Italian Riviera. This occurred shortly after one of the firm's clients announced the discovery of oil on 200,000 acres of its property. Upon investigation, it appeared that our departing messengers had purchased 400,000 shares of the client's stock two days before the oil discovery was announced, and sold the shares within the week. On learning of this, as the member of our corporate department responsible for SEC matters, I sprang into action immediately to protect client confidentiality by drafting an airtight Policy on Confidentiality of Information and Securities Investments. Our department circulates this policy eight times a year to everyone at the firm and requires that each person acknowledge the policy and swear to abide by it. Set forth below is that policy:

Policy on Confidentiality of Information and Securities Investments

General

Maintaining the confidentiality of our clients' proprietary information is perhaps the most important thing we do, although drafting contracts and litigating are pretty high up there on the list, too. Unlike our firm, which pretends that everything is confidential, some of our clients may actually have proprietary information that is worth protecting. In addition, the securities laws impose important restrictions on "insiders" of public companies with respect to their securities transactions. An "insider" is anybody on this planet who learns anything about a company that is not plastered on billboards.

The principal restriction on insiders is that they may not buy or sell securities on the basis of material information known to them but not to the public, or "tip" others concerning such information. (NOTE: this restriction has been held not to prohibit cash gratuities in restaurants, especially when 15% is automatically added to the check for parties of six or more.) The restriction on insider trading is extremely unfortunate because it's hard to get rich practicing law these days, and thus trading on inside information would be a terrific way to make a few quick bucks. But since violation of this restriction can carry criminal as well as treble-damage civil penalties, and the Securities and Exchange Commission's enforcement in this area is especially vigorous, we'd better watch our step. The guidelines and prior clearance procedures set forth in this policy memorandum are designed to protect you from violating these restrictions.

The nature of our practice is such that *all firm personnel* (partners and associates, as well as all those other, less important people floating around here) should be continually mindful of the necessity of maintaining the confidentiality of client information as well as the problems of insider trading. This memorandum sets forth and confirms how much the firm has always despised and been revolted at the mere thought of insider trading or inappropriate disclosure of confidential information.

Securities encompass a broad array of varying types of investments, including, but not limited to, stocks, whether common or uncommon; bonds; and limited partnership interests. In fact, one of the members of the corporate department thinks he remembers from his law school securities course that a cow can under certain circumstances be a security. Therefore, avoid trading heifers based on inside information, too. Because the securities laws are comprehensive, far-reaching, constantly evolving, and darn near inscrutable, this memorandum does not attempt to deal with all the considerations which may be applicable to an insider's securities transactions. That's your problem. Any questions you may have in this area should be directed to Alphonse Proust or some other member of the corporate department, who will bill you for their advice at their current hourly rate.

A. Persons Covered

It is important to emphasize that all firm personnel are covered by the policies set forth in this memorandum, however insignificant they may otherwise be, in whatever capacity they may work. These policies also apply to spouses, cousins, neighbors, casual acquaintances and any other people who might reasonably be deemed to have a relationship (legal, personal or otherwise) meriting coverage. Because this is so, all references contained in Sections B through F, inclusive, of this memorandum to firm personnel include all of these other people also.

B. Confidentiality

1. General Principle

It shall be the duty of each person employed by or affiliated with the firm to maintain top secret all information belonging or relating to the firm's clients and to protect that information with his or her life.

2. What Kind of Information Is Covered?

Set forth in Sections C.2. and 3. below is a brief discussion of "inside information" and "material information" in the context of "insider trading" and "tipping." The kind of information that may merit confidential treatment could be, and probably is, a whole lot broader, however. The best rule of thumb to follow is this: don't talk about anything to anybody.

3. What Steps Should Be Taken to Preserve Confidentiality?

You should take every impracticable step you can to preserve the confidentiality of confidential information. For example,

(a) Don't discuss confidential matters in restrooms (gents or gals) or any other place where you may be overheard.

(b) Don't read confidential documents in public places or discard them where they can be retrieved by bag ladies, who are notorious violators of the securities laws. Drafts of sensitive documents being discarded should be shredded or otherwise mutilated beyond recognition.

(c) Don't carry confidential documents in elevators, hallways, etc., in an exposed manner, or drop them like a clod where others could see them.

(d) Because of the carrying quality of conversations and the poor soundproofing in our offices, conduct all business in a whisper.

(e) Don't leave confidential documents in unattended conference rooms when the conference is over, since cleaning services are second only to bag ladies and Michael Milken as securities violators.

(f) Install a safe in your office and lock all confidential documents in it whenever you leave the room. The supply department has small sticks of dynamite available for use when you forget the combination to the safe. Please notify Chief Fitzpatrick prior to blasting.

(g) Code names should be used for matters involving material non-public information. Suggested code names are "Desert Storm," "Operation Rescue," and "Remember the Alamo."

Obviously, a list such as this can only be suggestive, so it is up to you to take whatever other impracticable steps are appropriate to preserve the confidentiality of confidential information.

C. Improper Insider Trading

1. General Prohibitions

An insider may not trade in securities on the basis of material inside information which has not been disclosed to the public. Neither may an insider give such information to another person—a "tippee"—who uses it for trading purposes. (Tippees should not be confused with Vice President Gore's wife, Tipper, but you can't tell her anything, either.)

Any firm personnel becoming aware that a person subject to this policy statement is about to trade at a time when the trading person is privy to material inside information relating to the company whose securities are to be traded should immediately so notify Alphonse Proust or, in his absence, the enforcement division of the SEC. Only kidding, don't ever call the SEC about anything.

2. What Is Inside Information?

Inside information includes anything learned as a result of a special relationship with the company. Since we have special relationships with all of our clients (though not as special as they once were), anything anyone knows at the firm about any client is inside information.

3. What Is Material Information?

The term "material information" has no precise or, for that matter, imprecise definition and is subject to roughly one hundred eighty-three thousand interpretations concerning the extent of its reach. For purposes of the firm's policies on insider trading, a ridiculously broad view of the term should be taken. Accordingly, "material information" should be considered to include:

(a) favorable horoscope of the chief financial officer;

(b) switch of the company's long distance carrier from AT&T to MCI;

(c) a lingering case of the flu in any officer paid more than $50,000 per year;

(d) the chief executive officer finding a lucky dime on the street (whether or not he picks it up); and

(e) the impending bar or bat mitzvah of the eldest child of any member of the board of directors.

4. When Is Information Deemed Public?

An insider may trade only when he is certain that official announcements of material information have been sufficiently publicized so that the public has had the opportunity to evaluate the information. To test whether information is public, stop three people at random on the street and ask them, "Did you hear about our client XYZ Corporation acquiring a $30 billion interest in the government of Saudi Arabia in exchange for a box of frisbees?" If all three have heard the news, the information is public and you may go right ahead and trade. If not, the information is not public, you may not trade and you should advise the people you have stopped on the street that they are "tippees" and that they should seek legal advice from our corporate department as to what the hell that means.

D. Investing in the Securities of Clients With Respect to Which the Firm Is Likely to Have Inside Dope

1. Policy

While the firm has not adopted an approach that would bar firm personnel from investing in publicly traded securities of clients, such investments raise difficult issues in the areas of disclosures, holding periods and the like. Accordingly, the firm believes that such investments can be permitted only in accordance with these guidelines, which are intended to be so onerous as to assure that nobody will invest in anything other than their piggybank.

2. Clearance Procedures

To avoid the appearance of impropriety, any purchase or sale of a security must be cleared in advance, as follows:

(a) Check the firm client list. If the client list indicates that the issuer of the securities is a client of the firm, you must then contact the partner in charge of that client. Unless and until you receive written clearance from that partner, you may not buy or sell any securities issued by that company under any circumstances.

(b) If the company is not on the client list, leave an E-mail message for every partner in the firm to make sure they don't know anything secret about the company. When everyone has E-mailed back their clearance, you may buy or sell stock, if the company is still in business.

This memorandum is distributed eight times a year, but we know that it is so gripping that you will read it anew each time. Not to frighten you or anything, but adhering to this policy's requirements is a material obligation of your continued employment at the firm.

I acknowledge that I have read and sorta understand the Fairweather, Winters & Sommers Policy on Confiden-

tiality of Information and Securities Investments, and I
agree to comply with its requirements, on penalty of death.

———————————

Signature

Questions Aired

WHENEVER difficult problems arise, the Fairweather firm turns to its prestigious consultants, Tellem, Wathey, Noh, for answers. In producing its reports, TWN designs custom surveys to aid it in analyzing the problem. Set forth below is a portion of the questionnaire utilized in connection with a recent TWN report.

Confidential Questionnaire

Instructions to those filling out questionnaire.

1. This questionnaire is completely confidential. We won't tell anybody your answers, no matter what—even if they try to bribe us, beat it out of us, or torture us by pulling out our fingernails or anything. We know that some people filling out a questionnaire like this might be afraid that their answers could lead to their being disciplined or fired. And, frankly, that's not such an irrational fear. Not with us, though. So just relax, your secret is safe with us. Mum's the word.

2. In filling out this questionnaire, use only a number two pencil, except that if you don't have a number two pencil, another pencil or even a pen will do. I mean, what's the big deal about using a number two pencil?

3. Read each question carefully, preferably before you answer it.

4. Answer every question. Select only one answer to each question. If you don't know the answer, take a wild stab at it. There are no deductions for incorrect answers, so it is to your advantage to guess.

5. Remember, this questionnaire is confidential. We really mean it.

6. Make heavy marks in the space to indicate your answer, or circle it or make a check or an X. Make no stray marks on this questionnaire; also, post no bills.

7. Be as frank and honest as you can in answering these questions. We'll find out the truth eventually, anyway.

8. No kidding: this questionnaire is confidential.

Personal Information

(NOTE: We need this information in order to correlate the data from the next section in a manner that is statistically significant and does not deviate from the mean regression in ways that would exceed N, where the distance from the moon is Y.)

1. Sex
   a. male
   b. female
   c. other
2. Race
   a. Caucasian
   b. Non-Caucasian
   c. 110-meter high hurdles
3. Height (in meters) ___
4. Weight (in stones) ___
5. Age (in weeks) ___
6. Favorite book _____
7. Sexual preference (please indicate first, second, and third choices)
   a. guys
   b. gals
   c. sheep
7. Favorite joke (use reverse side if necessary)
8. Most embarrassing moment

Non-personal Information

(NOTE: Some of these questions may appear not to relate to the subject being studied or to the questions before or after them. That is because this survey has been designed in such a sophisticated manner that you can't possibly understand what is going on. So don't worry about it, just answer the damn questions.)

1. My understanding of the mission of the firm is:
   a. to promote the ends of justice
   b. to promote the middle of justice
   c. to form a more perfect union
   d. to make money for the partners
   e. impossible

2. If John was four years older than Sally when Sally was one-third John's age, and John has recently attained the age at which it is legal to drink in his state (though John has been drinking beer since he was twice the age of Sally), then how long will it take Sally to get to John's house, driving at the legal speed limit, assuming that she hits only two red lights?
   a. not enough information given in the question to answer
   b. too much information given in the question to answer
   c. I'd say about twenty minutes, if traffic is not too heavy
   d. Sally is too young to have a driver's license
   e. none of the above

3. Which of the following would do most to increase the firm's profitability?
   a. reduce accounts receivable
   b. ignore accounts payable
   c. increase hourly billing rates

    d. charge lawyers for coffee

    e. redefine the term "hour" to mean "forty minutes"

4. The firm's reputation in the legal community is:

    a. top flight

    b. about at the second landing

    c. better than most

    d. not as high as it should be

    e. I'd just as soon not say

5. My opinion of Stanley J. Fairweather is:

    a. He is a god.

    b. He partakes of godly elements, but may not technically be a god.

    c. He is the most outstanding human being I have ever encountered.

    d. He is the most outstanding lawyer I have ever encountered.

    e. None of the above; I don't plan to remain at the firm long, anyway.

6. Lexis is:

    a. a computerized legal research system

    b. a luxury foreign automobile

    c. part of the name for somebody who confuses the order of numbers or letters

    d. more than one law (Lat.)

    e. all of the above

7. Draw a picture of your conception of an ideal law firm (let your imagination wander somewhat, but not too much; remember, you *are* a lawyer).

8. Which best characterizes feedback to associates:

    a. if you don't hear anything, you're doing fine

    b. if you don't hear anything, you're in trouble

    c. if you don't hear anything, you're either doing fine or in trouble

    d. if you receive positive feedback, you're either doing fine or are in trouble

    e. if you receive negative feedback, lay low, turn in your time sheets, and chances are good you'll make partner, anyway

9. If I were selected chair of the Executive Committee, I would:

    a. wonder what I'd done wrong to deserve this

    b. call my mother to tell her, right away

    c. seek to improve the firm's profitability

    d. double my compensation to where it should be

    e. resign and restore Stanley Fairweather to his rightful position

10. Which is the most important characteristic the firm should be seeking in its new lawyers:

    a. high IQ

    b. low maintenance

    c. high boredom threshold

    d. low sleep requirement

    e. high octane

11. I would describe the atmosphere at the firm as:

    a. ideal

    b. oppressive

    c. dull

    d. competitive

    e. humid

12. Write an essay on your summer vacation without using the word "notwithstanding."

13. Select the letter below which most closely parallels Stanley Fairweather: paralegal.

    a. cook: ladle

    b. ocean: puddle

    c. Shaquille O'Neal: Spud Webb

    d. prince: toad

    e. Zeus: thunderbolt

14. Pick the word from column B that is the antonym of the word in column A.

Column A	Column B
Stanley J. Fairweather	illegal pad
paralegal	interesting stuff
ERISA	I don't get it
legal pad	consensus-seeker
res ipsa loquitur	paracriminal

When you have completed this questionnaire, please forward it to Stanley Fairweather, as he would like to look these over before sending them on to us.

The Greening of Fairweather, Winters & Sommers

by Evelyn Lemker

TO DEMONSTRATE the firm's concern for the environment, we established the Fairweather Committee on Environmental Concerns on Earth Day 1990. For reasons I think you'll understand, I'd like to share with you a transcript of a portion of a recent meeting:

"I'm going to rule that suggestion out of order," said committee chair Beverly Post-Humous.

"Out of order? Why?" asked Sheldon Horvitz.

"Because it's beyond the jurisdiction of our committee," said the chair.

"That's ridiculous, we're the Committee on Environmental Concerns, aren't we?"

"Of course," conceded the chair.

"Well, birds are part of the environment, so why can't this committee propose that our firm choose a firm bird?" argued Sheldon.

"Well, no other firm has a firm bird," said committee member Seymour Plain.

"So much the better. That just proves that the Fairweather firm is in the vanguard of environmental concerns."

"Next thing you know you're going to be suggesting a firm flower," said Beverly.

"I was thinking of the snapdragon," said Sheldon.

"Look, Sheldon," said committee member Garrison Phelps, "even if we were going to choose a firm bird, we would not want to pick the spotted owl."

"And why not? It's an endangered species."

"Right, and one of our biggest clients is Logroller Lumber International, so if we pick the spotted owl as our firm bird, this law firm's going to become an endangered species."

"Well, I happen to think that we've got to have some principles, we can't just kowtow to narrow client interests."

"Sheldon, we're not the damn Audobon Society, you know. We're just a law firm trying to do its little piece for the environment. So I think we ought to stick with things like our recycling program."

"How is that program doing?" asked Seymour.

"Pretty well, except a dispute has developed regarding the cans."

"What kind of dispute? Do we have lawyers who don't want to recycle their cans?"

"No, it's not that; it's an economic issue. The dispute is over who is entitled to the refunds on the cans. Several partners have been keeping track of the number of cans they contribute and demanding that the refund be added to their capital accounts. The Finance Committee argues that the refund should go to the firm generally, since the firm provided the opportunity to purchase the cans and also bears the overhead associated with recycling."

"Is there that much money involved? I can't imagine that any partner would be interested in the deposit."

"Well, Nails Nuttree says that he drinks an average of four Mountain Dews a day. At five cents a can, he figures that comes to twenty cents a day, a dollar a week, or fifty dollars a year. Over a twenty-year period, that's a thousand dollars, not including the soft drinks that his guests consume. So we're starting to get into real money here."

"Well, I assume the Executive Committee will resolve that one eventually."

"Yes, with an emphasis on the eventually. They've already discussed the issue at three meetings, and the EC vote breaks down along the lines of heavy and light Diet Coke consumers."

"Speaking of recycling, how is our effort to use recyclable paper for our stationery going?"

"We're making some progress."

"What is that supposed to mean?"

"Well, we've overcome the initial concerns. The cost is somewhat higher than our regular stationery was, but we found a bidder whose price is close enough for us to absorb the difference. And though some lawyers don't like the look and feel of the paper, we think we've finally identified a high-quality recyclable paper that will satisfy everyone."

"Great, then what's the hang-up?"

"The Executive Committee is balking at our suggestion that the bottom of each sheet of stationery contain the legend, 'This stationery is another project of the Committee on Environmental Concerns, printed on recyclable paper in order to preserve our dwindling rainforests and dryforests.'"

"What's their problem?"

"They're afraid that between the letterhead with everyone's name on it and the legend we're proposing on the bottom of the sheet, there'll be no room for the body of the letter."

"Well, that's easy. Why don't we just get rid of all the names at the top of the letterhead?"

"You're probably too young to remember what happened the last time somebody proposed that."

"What happened?"

"The Executive Committee spent four months on the topic."

"How did they eventually resolve it?"

"They decided to get rid of the letterhead, but they grandpersoned every living partner in, so that the change will not take effect until some time deep into the twenty-first century."

"What about our other projects? How is our Plant-a-Tree-for-Fairweather Program for lawyers' kids coming?"

"Very well, we now have a veritable forest budding in Lincoln Park."

"And did we get permission from the Finance Committee for the firm to adopt a highway?"

"Not exactly; it was too expensive. But they did agree to allow us to adopt a side street near Stanley's house, and we are scheduled to send a crew out to clean the street next month."

"Our pro bono efforts on behalf of environmental concerns are progressing quite well, too," reported Sheldon. "We are suing the governments of Japan and Russia on behalf of Save the Whales, and we have a team traveling around Central and South America trying to protect a rare strain of mute parrots."

"Aren't those efforts costing the firm a fortune?"

"What's a fortune? And, in any case, what are a few bucks compared to our grandchildren's quality of life?"

"What have our grandchildren done for us recently?"

"Never mind. Besides, all of this is a big help to us in our recruitment efforts. Some of the best students in law school these days are interested in saving the environment."

"That's wonderful. We'll get them here and they'll be

invaluable in helping us pursue our pro bono work, then find out that they can't expect to do it full-time and draw a salary, and wind up leaving our firm for one of our competitors who do no pro bono work at all."

"Now, Garrison, you sound as if you're not four-square behind our pro bono efforts for the environment."

"It's not that. It's just that we've got so many activities going on in our Committee on Environmental Concerns, it's getting very difficult to keep track of them all."

"I agree, and it's taking up too much lawyer time besides."

"Fortunately I've got just the answer," announced Sheldon.

"You always do," said Seymour. "What is it this time?"

"I think we need to hire a full-time director of environmental concerns to help us keep track of and coordinate all of our environmental activities."

"Wonderful, Sheldon. Try selling that one to the Finance Committee."

"That should be an absolute cinch."

"How do you figure that?"

"Well, the Finance Committee is interested in reducing costs, right?"

"Of course."

"Well, just look at all of the lawyer time we're spending administering our environmental concern activities. I figure that hiring a full-time director may be one of the biggest cost-saving moves our firm could make this year."

*   *   *

So that's how my position came to be. Of course, as our brand new director of environmental concerns, I don't have much to report yet on our activities. I want to say that I'm enthusiastic about Sheldon's suggestion of adopting a firm bird, though I differ with him on which bird we should choose. The spotted owl, I'm afraid, is on its way out. So why not pick one that's likely to be around forever, and would fit in well with the firm's historical management style — the hummingbird; it flies backwards.

Conclusion

SOME OF MY FRIENDS got wind of the fact that this book was in the works, and asked me why in the dickens I would let it happen. I told them I was letting it happen because the book seemed to me to be a damn good idea.

They asked me, "Why?" (Persistent little cusses, aren't they? I'm not used to being asked "why" around my firm.)

But knowing me, I was quite confident that I had a good reason why, so I decided to figure out what that reason was. And, as it turns out, I had five pretty good reasons:

1. The book means publicity for the firm, and I'm a strong adherent to the view that any publicity is good, as long as they spell my name correctly.

2. Publishing the book will give recognition to lots of folks on the support staff who have made a big contribution to my firm over the years. That's good.

3. Writing the book will give folks around the firm something to do, which is the same reason I set up all of those committees you've read about in T*he Handbook of Law Firm Mismanagement* and *Advanced Law Firm Mismanagement* (and, come to think of it, you've read about a few of them in here, too).

4. The firm's going to make some money on the book and, though my partners and I are unlikely to retire on the royalties, every little bit helps.

5. But the most important reason for publishing this book is this—to honor disorganization. In fact, maybe we

should have called this thing *The Handbook of Law Firm Disorganization*. You see, I believe strongly that disorganization has its place. Excessive organization stifles. And out of disorganization often is borne creativity, as you may have noticed in this book.

Now, I would be the first to admit that we at the Fairweather firm may have overdone our disorganization a bit. But at least that gives us something towards which to strive in the future—the perfect level of disorganization.